Other Books by Michael Panno

Animal Rites
Shocks & Bar-B-Q

Down Clark Street

© Primordial Press
A division of Uprising Communications Group
P.O. Box 490
Laguna Beach, CA 92652

Copyright © 2013 by Michael Panno
Cover design by Studio Productions and Michael Panno
Cover Photo by Nancy (Panno) Eden
Author photo by Lauren Panno
Library of Congress Catalog Card Number 2013909460
ISBN: 978-0967785929

First Edition

UPRISING

Down Clark Street
Michael Panno

Primordial Press
Laguna Beach

One of the signs of passing youth is the birth of a sense of fellowsip with other human beings as we take our place among them.

Virginia Woolf

for
Aliyah and Aminah

PROLOGUE

I remember waking one winter morning to the sound of children playing outside my window, their small voices ascending like spirits, briefly tapping against our window and then drifting away. I shared a bed with my brother, Frank, on the second floor of the house—more of a large landing than a bedroom—overlooking our front yard.

Though this was not the first time others had beaten me to a fresh snow, it was the first time my tardiness had brought with it any anxiety, as if, unlike before, something irretrievable had been lost. Children were at play, laughing, singing; a fresh snow had fallen. Life was abundant and I had somehow slept through a small portion of it.

I gazed down at Frank—fast asleep. In the corner, in a heap, were our clothes: the heavy winter coat handed down from Frank to me, the leather gloves worn thin at the fingertips. A soft light twisted its way up the staircase, probably from the kitchen. I listened for sounds of life within our house; all was quiet.

I got up from the bed and went to the window. The faces below were familiar. Their voices grew fainter as the sound of my own heart drowned them out. I was eleven years old and though I didn't realize it then, I was beginning to mark time.

ONE

My parents' sixth and last child—a boy—was born the last week of November 1958, two weeks premature, weighing in at just a little under five pounds. A few days later, having reached five pounds and deemed well enough to discharge, he arrived home by way of my father's cab.

My sister Mary and I were in the backyard on our swings when they arrived. We had wiped away an inch of fresh snow, chipped off a layer of ice beneath it, and then wrapped some old towels around the faded yellow seats in an effort to diminish the cold. Before us, on the ground, was a three-foot mound of snow, sculpted by the two of us and strategically located to serve as a cushion for our daredevil leaps into space.

Our white Adirondack chairs sat like three fat men knee deep in snow beneath the huge oak tree in the middle of our yard, icicles descending from their arms like unkempt fingernails. I had watched in envy the previous summer as my dad and my older brother, Frank painted them, Frank haphazardly slopping on the paint, my father admonishing his lethargic effort.

"I can help," I said, not so much because I wanted to do the work but rather to offer them both a way out of this entanglement before it got any worse.

"Yeah, let Mike do it," said Frank.

My father took a deep breath, stopped his brush in mid-stroke and turned to Frank. "Just paint. Mike's too young."

Frank was thirteen, just three years older than me, hardly enough in my mind to selectively qualify him for the job. He was, I admit, quite a bit taller than me, and stronger, but it was, after all, just a paintbrush. And I also didn't understand why my Dad had Frank help him in the first place. They didn't get along. When that all started, I couldn't say—it just always seemed to be that way—and why it was, well that was also a mystery.

But there they were once again, butting heads. They seemed less like father and son and more like two kids in a schoolyard scrap. They didn't even look alike. My father was Sicilian, brown—well, mostly grey now—curly hair, dark complexion with eyes like coal, short in stature with a bit of a paunch developing as he entered middle age. Frank took after my mother's side of the family. She was German and Irish, and Frank had inherited those traits: the straight, dark hair, full lips, strong chin and a healthy dose of independence. Perhaps that was it. Perhaps my father looked at Frank and didn't recognize him, saw only a stranger, a stranger trying to stake a claim on a piece of ground right under my father's feet, a stranger who, like the rest of the outside world, would give my father little quarter.

"How old do you have to be to paint a stupid chair?"

"I can do it," I said.

My father dropped his brush into the can. His hands were covered with paint and when he reached up to wipe some sweat from his face, he left a few white spots on his nose, which he must have been able to see, for he quickly grabbed a rag and began rubbing away at them, his eyes crossing in the process.

"Why don't you both just get the hell out of my hair so I can get this finished," he said and stuck the rag in his back pocket.

"Fine with me," said Frank, who then tossed the brush onto one of the chairs and shuffled away.

"Hey, where you going?" my father yelled after him. "Get back here!" But Frank just kept moving as I stood gawking at the unmanned brush. I wanted him to invite me to pick it up. I waited for some kind of sign, a look, but he merely continued to curse Frank's departure as he returned to the work at hand. I stood in silence for a few minutes and then quietly walked away.

———

"I'm getting cold," said Mary.

"We just got out here," I said as I pumped for more height. The snow was deep and packed solid around the legs but it could not hold the rickety old swing set in place, the poles lifting up an inch or so with each ascent of the swing.

Despite being twins, the two of us looked nothing alike. Mary had jet black hair like my Aunt Rose, and fair skin. I was darker skinned, like my father, and I also had his brown wavy hair. In fact, I had been told that he looked just like me when he was a kid. Mary and I were close in size, but I did have about an inch on her, an all-important inch at age eleven. We shared the same large dark-brown eyes and a certain sensitivity to the world around us, a sensitivity I worked at controlling so as to separate my identity from hers. It was not an easy task.

"I can't help it," she said. "I'm cold."

"Just don't think about it," I said as I bailed out from the swing, my timing slightly off—I'm sure I blamed her for the distraction—causing me to land just short of the white cushion, onto the frozen earth.

I rolled over on my side and grabbed my left knee.

"Are you alright?" she asked and released from her swing into the pile. A splatter of snow swept across my face.

"Are you alright?" She brushed herself off and came to my side.

"I'm fine," I said, more for myself than her, tears gathering quickly in the corners of my eyes. I brought a sleeve up to wipe them away, covering my face with still more snow in the process, got to my feet, my right leg carrying most of the weight, brushed the snow from my body and limped over to the swing.

I started pumping.

Mary got back on her swing. "Peter McBride said he can go all the way around if he gets up enough speed," she said.

"He can not."

"Said he could."

"Lots of people say things; doesn't make them true. Haven't you heard of a thing called gravity?"

"What about Ferris wheels? They go all the way around."

"That's different."

"Why?"

"It just is. They have motors and stuff, and metal spokes."

I was building quite a bit of momentum on my swing, to the point where at the apex I could feel the tautness loosen in the chain and for just a split second experience the unnerving thrill of weightlessness. At these heights, unencumbered with weight, the mind ran free; anything seemed possible. Suspended in time and space, all things were equal; the chairs, trees, house, snow, all stuck to the Earth, their only chance of escape was to melt, rust or slowly chip away. Perhaps, I thought, Peter was right. I imagined myself floating over the top of the swing set, lighter than smoke, free to drift haphazardly above a nailed down world.

The chain from my swing jerked abruptly as I began my descent, snapping me out of my reverie. I reached bottom, then proceeded to climb again toward the back of the swing, finally reaching eye level with the crossbar atop the set.

I could see a section of our gravel driveway—now covered with snow—leading up to the nursery my parents had built. They had hoped it would be a moneymaker and allow my mother to quit her job at the hospital, but it never quite panned out. Sometimes she'd have seven or eight kids for a month or two and she would cut back to part time at the hospital, but then there would be a layoff at the bottle factory or a particularly nasty flu virus would hit and all of a sudden she'd be down to one or two kids. She still took kids in on weekends, but for the most part the small building became more of a playroom for us.

My parents had even put our RCA Victor Radio in there. When I was around six or seven I would sit by myself in our living room and listen to baseball games, or country music. There was a show that came out of Chicago—Randy Blake and the Supper Time Frolics—that played all the greats: Hank Snow, Hank Williams, Ray Price. Red Sovine had a tune called Why Baby Why?, and I remember driving everyone in the house crazy with my rendition of it. "Why baby, why. Why baby, why," I'd sing, over and over, repeating just those two words. About the time I'd get one song out of my head and everyone thought their suffering was over, I'd start in with another. "Hey, good lookin' what you got cookin'..." It got to the point where the minute I'd turn on the Frolics, everybody would vacate the room, except for my father, who would listen closely for a few tunes, make a comment about "hillbilly music" and then quietly disappear. It wasn't until rock & roll came around that they finally moved the radio into the nursery. Whether that was a coincidence or if Jerry Lee Lewis was the final straw, I really couldn't say.

My father's yellow taxi turned into the drive and Mary yelled out. "It's them!"

They arrived, a jerky scenario, clicked off like snapshots each time I reached the top: an open door; Frank; my mother (thinner now, with baby in hand); my father (his dingy yellow hat falling to the ground as he exited the cab); the screen door to the porch, suspended—like me—then shut; smoke pouring from the exhaust pipes as the weathered taxi shivered in the wind, and then my father returning, picking up his hat, getting into the cab and driving away.

Mary was half way to the house before I hit the ground. I followed her through the porch door, leaving it slightly ajar as I entered, and stomped my way through the porch in an effort to release the abundant snow from my jeans and boots before reaching the dining room. The door separating the two rooms was open wide, one pane of glass still missing from the previous summer when Frank and I broke it during a wrestling match.

I burst through. "Where is it?" I said and squeezed in between Mary and my mother against the large oak dining table.

"He," said my older sister, Carol, "is not an it."

The room was small and sparsely furnished: a small curio cabinet in one corner that held a few cups, dishes and a heavy serving plate (all of these were of the same design: white with tiny red roses around the edges, left to my mother from her mother); a Singer sewing machine with a black metal foot pedal; and the oak table, complete with eight chairs. The floor was oak, like our table, but worn and without luster and covered almost entirely by a braided oval rug.

In the center of the table was a small bassinet and from within it came a light whimper. I stood on my tiptoes trying to see. "I can't see it," I said.

"He's not an it," said Mary.

"Midget," said Frank.

"All of you be quiet," said my mother. "Mary, you and Michael can get up on a chair so you can see better. Frank, don't tease your brother."

Frank flicked me in the side of the head with his finger. I pushed his hand away and climbed up on a chair next to Mary. There in the middle of the bassinet lay our newest addition, squirming and kicking and grappling for his share of space. I looked toward my mother but she was all his. A cool draft raced through the room and she lifted the baby from the bassinet and held him close. He sneezed and she blessed him as she folded the blanket to his chin.

His skin was all red and wrinkled, his eyes hidden behind quivering lids.

"He's so cute," said Mary.

"He looks kind of ugly to me," I said.

"What do you think you looked like?" said Frank.

"Not like that! I was cute, wasn't I mom?"

"You were all cute when you were babies," she said. "And a lot less ornery."

Mary reached up and poked the baby gently in the stomach.

"You sure made up for it though," said Frank.

Again the cold air whipped through the room and my mother turned toward the open door.

"Why is that door open?"

Everyone looked at me.

"I didn't do it," I said, but quickly jumped down from my chair and ran to the porch, retracing my wet tracks back to the exterior door, which had also been left ajar.

I stood in that open doorway watching the falling snow—the clouds darker now and closer to the ground—then stuck my head outside in an attempt to catch a flake on my tongue. I recalled someone telling me that each snowflake was unique, had its own design; but they all tasted the same to me, simply wet and bland. I wondered how anyone would know they were all different from each other without having seen every snowflake that ever fell to Earth.

The tire tracks from my father's cab were slowly filling in with snow; his footprints had practically disappeared.

"Michael!" my mother's voice called out.

I drew in my tongue, shut the door and ran back to the dining room, closing the second door behind me.

"Sorry," I said. "It's snowing pretty hard."

"Can I hold him?" asked Carol as she came around the table to my mother's side. She handed him to Carol, and Frank looked at me and rolled his eyes.

"Be careful," she said.

"What are you going to name him?" asked Mary.

"Martin."

"By all means," said Frank. Let's do our bit for the church."

"Frank," said my mother, as if he were belaboring a dead issue.

I turned to Frank. "What?"

"Don't you know the deal?"

"What deal?"

"A house full of saints."

My mother glared at Frank. "Frank, just leave it alone."

I heard the back door open and then the unmistakable voice of Mrs. Grady call out. "Hello. Helen."

"In here," said my mother.

Mrs. Grady hobbled in. She was carrying what looked like a pie in one hand, and in the other she held a plain wooden cane. She had broken her hip a year earlier and when she walked her left side would rise up above her right. My friend Peter said she looked like she had a turd in her pants.

She was in her sixties, grey hair, which she wore in a bun and wrapped with a scarf, a plain, ankle length housedress buttoned to the chin, dark socks and heavy dark shoes, the only skin revealed being that of her weathered face and hands.

She had been recently widowed and, although somewhat of a busybody and perpetually grumpy, was always welcome in our house. She did not like winter for it deprived her of her greatest pleasure: working in her garden; and her garden was everywhere. There were roses, violets, carnations, rows of tomatoes, lettuce, carrots, and rhubarbs, to name a few. Even the space between our houses was utilized for a bed of tulips, and we were absolutely forbidden to pass through it, even though it was our yard.

"Thought I heard your car," she said, moving close to the table and setting the pie on it. "Made you a rhubarb pie. So that's him, huh. What's he weigh?"

"Seven pounds," said my mother. It was a lie, uttered in an attempt to ward off what we all knew was coming next.

"Don't look like seven," said Mrs. Grady. "Looks more like six. You got to watch him close, make sure he gets plenty to eat. And keep him warm. Don't want to catch pneumonia in this weather."

"I'll try and remember that, Margaret," said my mother.

The irony went right past Mrs. Grady, or at least she did not let on if she had gotten the message. She had no children of her own, but on this and most other matters, she considered herself an expert.

Frank moved close to Carol and peered over her shoulder. "Training?"

"You're so immature."

"You're so immature," said Frank, mimicking her.

"Okay, Frank, that's enough. Out. Go on."

"Fine with me," said Frank. He grabbed me by the arm and pulled me with him. "Come on. Let's go sledding."

"No sledding," said my mother. "It's almost dinner time."

"Okay, Helen," said Frank. He had just recently begun calling my mother by name and only when he wanted to make the point that she was bugging him. It didn't seem to bother her; in fact, I think she liked it. It was like their own little private joke. Sometimes she'd fire back with "I'll Helen you," or "don't get smart with me," but it was always followed by a laugh.

Frank turned to me. "I'll get my BB gun. We'll go downstairs."

"No BB gun in the cellar," said my mother.

"What's the big deal?" asked Frank.

My mother took a deep breath and glared at Frank. "I'm the bid deal, Frank. No gun in the cellar."

"Great," said Frank.

"I could pitch some to you," I said.

"We did that yesterday."

"I need to be ready for Little League tryouts."

"That's six months away."

I shrugged my shoulders.

"Fine," said Frank. "Go get your stuff."

The two of us started to leave the room. "Hey, maybe we can go to Clark Street tomorrow," I said.

"Maybe," said Frank. "I think they closed it off today."

My mother called out to us. "Don't be too long down there…and check the furnace."

"Yes, Helen" said Frank and we left the four females there in the dining room, cooing and poking at the newest arrival.

TWO

I woke early the next morning to the sound of Martin crying—a high pitched complaint, all dry and staccato—and went immediately to the window. It must have snowed all night; the driveway, the sidewalk, the bottom step to the porch—all had disappeared. My warm breath fogged the window so I undid the latch and pushed it up a few inches. Cold air rushed in and with it the sounds of winter: the boisterous complaint of a hungry blue jay, the squirrels' chatter, the final groans of a dying car battery.

Across the street, George Price and another boy were knee deep trying to build a snowman, but the snow was still too fresh and powdery to stick. Our yard had not yet been violated by child or beast and I felt torn between leaving it that way and getting out in it. But then, children have no taste for preserving moments or savoring the unspoiled.

I shut the window, returned to the bed and shook Frank. He pulled the covers over his head and rolled over onto his stomach. I tried again. "Frank. Frank, get up. Let's go outside."

"Go away."

"But the snow's really deep. Let's go to Clark Street."

He grabbed a pillow and put it over his head and I gave up. I heard a new noise, a coarse, scraping sound, and returned to the window. A passing tractor cleared the street, its heavy metal plow scraping the brick road and depositing a wall of dirty snow like a festering wound across the front of our yard. My father had likewise begun clearing our driveway, his wide shovel blazing a trail to the street, and disrupting the virgin field of snow.

I pulled away from the window and quickly dressed, then climbed over the balustrade onto the two-inch ledge, leaning backward over the staircase as I inched my way along toward the top step. It was a trick I had mastered playing tag—an escape route. Frank had even, on occasion, swung over and dropped straight down into the stairwell, landing halfway down the steps. I wasn't quite ready for that.

Carol came out of the girls' bedroom and saw me. "You're gonna break your neck one of these days."

At the sound of her words, I let go of one hand and extended one leg out into mid-air above the staircase and began singing. "It's a long way to the bottom, it's a long way to the floor..."

"You'll be singing another tune if that banister breaks. I'm telling mom."

"Go ahead. You're just jealous 'cause your too chicken to do it."

"I'm trying to sleep, you guys!" yelled Frank from under his pillow. Carol lowered her voice a little.

"Get off of there, Michael, right now," she said as she started down the steps.

I pulled myself to the railing and quickly scooted toward the steps, then jumped to the third one from the top, right in front of her. "Beat you downstairs," I said, as I hurried down the steps.

Downstairs had the all too familiar aroma of cinnamon and vanilla, which meant oatmeal...again. I sat next to the radiator on the dining room floor and grabbed my rubber boots—the bottom two buckles still hooked shut from the day before, my tennis shoes trapped inside—loosened the buckles and removed the shoes—still damp—and carefully placed them beside the radiator to dry. (Once, I accidentally left a boot on the register only to have it melt and stink up the house for hours.) It had all the makings outside for a two-pair-of-shoes day. I pulled the boots over my second pair of tennies and walked into the kitchen.

"Hi, mom." She had on the new slippers she'd bought for her stay at the hospital and the familiar terry-cloth robe which she tied off just above her stomach, still swollen from the pregnancy. Her hair was shoulder length, brown, tied loosely in a ponytail to keep it out of her face while she cooked. At forty, her face was still wrinkle-free, her complexion as smooth and pure as the day she left the farm. Only her eyes betrayed her age.

"Michael, if I catch you hanging over that banister, you're gonna get your butt blistered."

I looked to Carol, who merely smirked and then turned away.

"It's not dangerous..."

"No. Well, I am," she said, and then turned from her stove to catch her first look at me as I zipped up my jacket. At this point in my life I still believed she was (dangerous), still held reverence for her authority. Frank, on the other hand, merely laughed at her commands or obeyed simply to humor her. It wasn't that he didn't love or respect her— they never fought—he had just emancipated himself from her and she, like any mother with good sense, did not try to stop it. Of course the ritual of command continued (old habits die hard) but there was no meat left to it. No, there was peace between Frank and Helen. The war was with my father.

From the dining room came a muffled sneeze.

"Carol, will you check on Martin?"

"Okay," she said and as she brushed by me I stuck out my tongue. My mother turned her attention to me.

"And you can just take off that jacket. You're not going anywhere until you eat your breakfast."

"But I'm not hungry and it snowed last night."

She set the large wooden spoon on the stove and began nudging me toward the dining room.

"Go on, get it off and go sit down; this is ready."

I walked out onto the porch, a cold room enclosed primarily by glass, and used only as an entrance during winter; a place to clean ones boots and leave behind whatever weather we'd collected. During the summer it helped keep the dining area cool in the morning, but of course once the sun got overhead the entire house would swelter in the heat and humidity.

I checked for my father's car but it was not in the driveway; fresh tracks led to the street. I left the room, being sure to close the porch door behind me. A cool draft funneled through the empty pane. I returned to the kitchen.

"Where's dad?"

"He went to church and then he's going to work."

"He said he'd give us a ride to Clark Street, and I told Peter we'd pick him up."

"Well, I guess you'll have to walk."

"He promised."

"Well, you should have gotten up earlier. You could have gone to church with him."

My father went to church almost every Sunday. For the

rest of us, somewhere along the line our attendance had slid into the optional category, which meant none of us—with the exception of Carol—hardly ever went.

I went into the dining room where Carol gently rocked Martin in her arms. She looked older than her seventeen years, and if seen in the street with Martin, could easily pass for his mother. This was due not so much to any premature aging on her part, but more the way she carried herself; the way she wore her hair—pulled back off her forehead with a headband—and the dark horn-rimmed glasses that took up way too much of her face. Unlike my mother, she had a very small bone structure and tiny features which gave her a frail look, where, in reality, she was very strong and healthy.

"Are you and Richard getting married?"

"Maybe, after we get out of school. Why?"

"Just wondered. How many more days till Christmas?"

"Three weeks."

"But how many days?"

"Well, what's three times seven?"

"Twenty-one. But is it exactly three weeks from today?"

"Look on the calendar," she said, slightly exasperated. "Why do you need to know, anyway?"

"Just wondered."

I took off my jacket and placed it on the back of a chair and sat down. Carol started talking to Martin—baby talk.

"Why do girls do that?"

My mother came into the room and set a bowl of oatmeal in front of me.

"Do what?" she said.

"Oh, you're so cute, you're so sweet. It's not like he can understand you."

"It's never too soon, Michael. Babies can tell by the tone

of your voice that you love them."

Mary came into the room, jacket in hand. "Can I go with you, today?"

"I'm going with Peter."

"Mom..." said Mary.

"Can't you take your sister with you?"

"She always complains she's too cold. Then I have to walk home with her." I stared into my bowl of oatmeal. "Do I have to eat all of this?"

"Yes, you do. Mary, why don't you stay home and help us with the baby, today."

I turned and looked at Mary. She had been born nine minutes after me and it seemed like she was always at my heels. She was slow getting ready for school in the morning (as if she could somehow stop time) and would often refuse to go. Then I'd have to sit and plead with her until finally she'd acquiesce and we'd end up having to run most of the way to avoid being late. She had been that way since second or third grade—some innate feeling she had about teachers or authority that made her rebel in any small way she could. To put it in a word, she was contrary. If a teacher said black, she said white; up was down, etc.

So we were late a lot and she missed a lot of days. My mother soon ran out of ideas for notes. Once, at St. Anthony's, we actually brought a note to school—composed by Mary—after missing half a day, wherein she explained we had been kept home that morning because our cheeks were red. I had my doubts about the note working and when Mary handed it to Sister Mary Elizabeth they were confirmed. She read it quietly to herself, then pinched Mary by the cheeks with her left hand, forcing her head to an upward position, and began shaking her right forefinger in Mary's face.

"If I see one more note like this," she said, "I'll give you some red cheeks." She turned to me. "Both of you."

There was a short outburst of laughter from the other children, but Sister grabbed her ruler and brought it down hard against her desk, and the room fell deadly quiet. I think we were seven years old at the time.

Things improved a little in public school, until fifth grade. That was the year we had Mrs. Patterson. An elderly woman without children of her own, she had dedicated her life to a profession least suited for her sensibilities, for she did not like children, particularly children who possessed any semblance of free spirit. While most of us got our revenge anonymously by drawing stick figures of her on the blackboard or putting dead creatures in her desk, Mary chose a more direct method. She would disagree with her in front of the whole class, questioning her point of view regarding a particular historical event, or attacking the virtue of the "literature" we were assigned to read. (She especially hated the Wild West books: Davy Crockett, Buffalo Bill, and Daniel Boone.)

Once, when she had been invited to the blackboard to show what she felt was the correct way to spell the word dispense—for spelling was her forte; she won all the bees—I extended a leg and tripped her. (I don't know why; it was just one of those foolish things kids do—an impulse.) She managed to brace herself and avoid hitting the ground, but the humiliation proved too much, for upon her arrival at the blackboard she was unable to correct Mrs. Patterson's abominable spelling of the word, wherein—as was her habit—she had replaced the *s* with a *c*.

She just stood there facing the blackboard—the laughter dying off into silent anticipation—and when at last she turned her head to look out at us, I couldn't meet her eyes.

"Well, Mary?" said Mrs. Patterson, and a very tight-lipped sardonic smile crossed her face. My brief moment of glory from the class's laughter was dampened by my feelings of shame for having inadvertently aligned myself with our teacher's cause, and as Mary returned to her seat I knew I had lost some small piece of her.

———

"You can come," I said, and forced down the final bite of my cereal; but it was too late.

"No, that's okay, I think I'll stay here with Martin."

"I don't mind," I said in a half-hearted attempt to change her mind.

"No, you're right, it's too cold. I'll stay here."

"Okay." I shrugged my shoulders, trying my best not to display either my feelings of guilt or relief. I got up from the table, picked up my empty bowl and took it into the kitchen, then quickly returned through the dining room, grabbed my jacket and said goodbye.

THREE

The McBrides lived at the corner, four doors down from us, in a small gray, one story house with clapboard siding, the paint long ago weathered away except for the occasional patch of white under the eaves. Sections of the porch banister were missing, as were many of the boards from the deck, and the entire first step. In the summer, Mr. McBride would sit out there for hours, his feet propped up on the railing, a beer always within reach. If you caught him early enough in the afternoon—while he was still somewhat sober—he might tell you a joke or use a word you never heard before, and then tell you not to tell your parents where you heard it because kids weren't supposed to use it. But the thing was, they didn't necessarily have to be curse words. They could be words as innocuous as swap, or guzzle, not particularly pleasing phonetically—and perhaps associated with somewhat questionable behavior—but definitely not words to cause our mothers to break out the soap. I don't know if he thought his secret words would endear him to us, or if his mind was just going.

Mrs. McBride I saw mostly in passing: Mrs. McBride on her way to the A & P (her day job); Mrs. McBride coming home from the A & P; Mrs. McBride on her way to the Cab Company (her night job); Mrs. McBride going for more beer.

In winter she wore a grey full-length wool coat, very plain with large black buttons, rubber boots with zippers rather than buckles, and a faded turquoise scarf that looked like it was very beautiful once upon a time. She never wore gloves; why that was I couldn't say, but I would see her walking in the middle of a snow storm without gloves, the rest of her protected from the elements head to toe, while her hands—very small hands as I recall—always exposed. In the summer she would of course go without the heavy coat or boots but the scarf was always there, tied loosely at the chin, locks of her black hair poking out around the edges. Always on foot, always a smile when she passed, rarely a word spoken, her life progressed like the hands of an old clock, each day running a little bit slower than the one before it.

She was a Cowen, disowned for marrying McBride. (Most people in town believed it was for getting pregnant by him that she was disinherited but according to my mother it was their marriage that undid her; the pregnancy brought shame upon her, of course, but for a Cowen to marry a McBride, well, that was just too much.) Perhaps she thought by doing the right thing she'd regain their good opinion of her; perhaps she loved him. Cut out of the family fortune, she now held a place no higher than a servant—without pay.

———

I stood up to my calves in snow, calling.

"Peter! Peter!"

I could hear voices inside, mostly that of Mr. McBride, gruff and violent, the words indiscernible. It was strange to hear him up and about this early in the day; he had lost his job at the canning factory a year before and now rarely stirred before noon. His drinking problem had become worse; at least when he had a job he kept sober during the day. And there had even been rumors of him occasionally hitting his wife. A couple of the drivers at the Yellow Cab had threatened to take matters into their own hands (Mrs. McBride was well liked; she was the best dispatcher they had), but Mrs. McBride managed to dissuade them. "I made this bed," she told them, "I can handle it."

Peter stuck his head out the door. "I'll be out in a minute," he said, the words whistling through the gap where once hung his two front teeth.

"Hurry up."

"I gotta get my boots on. Just wait a minute."

He closed the door and once again I could hear the other voices, but less frequent now like the contractions of cooling metal.

I dug down below the fresh snow in search of some that would pack better and managed to make a decent snowball. There was a large, bald elbow on one of the branches of the elm tree that spread over half the McBride's roof. I wound up and delivered a fastball, dead center.

"Strike!" I yelled out and dug into the snow for another ball. Once again I hit my target and once again called out.

"Strike two!" A squirrel stuck its head around the tree and into the strike zone. I prepared another ball.

"Mantle steps up to the plate. Drysdale looks in for the sign. Shakes one off, and another. Gets the one he's looking for and fires."

The snowball exploded one inch in front of the squirrel's nose and he quickly darted away.

"That'll teach you to crowd the plate on me."

Peter shuffled out the front door, his jacket half way on, his hat and gloves in hand.

"I gotta get my sled," he said and ran around to the side of the house.

Peter's sled was in just as ill repair as the house he lived in. The runners were rusty from neglect and one of the handles was broken, forming a somewhat jagged weapon and making steering rather difficult. Even the clothesline he used to drag it along behind him was about to snap.

I don't recall where my sled came from, though I know I didn't get it new. (If you wanted something new in our house you had to give birth to it.) I did, however, keep it in good repair, kept the rails greased and the wood varnished— with Frank's help of course.

"Took you long enough," I said as he came around the corner, the old sled sliding along behind him. His hair was red, long and shaggy, and protruded from the edges of his leather cap, one of those with the padded earflaps. He always turned the flaps down, but never buttoned the strap. His jeans had been patched in numerous spots (he wore two pair), his coat an old Navy pea coat (his father's) that came down to his knees; the sleeves had been tucked under and sewn but still dropped down to the middle of his hands. His boots were just like mine. If it weren't for his boyish complexion, he might very well have passed for a short, stocky sailor, fresh off the boat.

"My old man wasn't gonna let me go."

"Why not?"

"I don't know. Says I woke him up. You know how he is. Let's get out of here before the old fart comes out."

We started down the street, two adventurers with the world laid out before us in a splendor of white powder. It seemed, in that moment, that anything was possible, that time was a friend, a slow moving beast lumbering patiently at our side.

"Whadaya wanna do?" said Peter.

"Frank said they had Clark Street closed yesterday. Said it was real fast."

Peter stopped. "That's too far. Let's just play chicken out on Monroe."

I reached deep into the snow, packed another ball and delivered it sidearm to the heart of an old garbage can. The can was empty and clanged against the one adjacent to it.

"Last time we played chicken, I smashed my fingers," I said. "You never turn, unless I do, and then you still try to smash into me."

In chicken, the two of us would approach each other at full speed on our sleds, the first one turning away being the chicken. Every eleven-year-old boy wants to think of himself as courageous and, even more importantly, to be thought so by his peers. I was no different, but what I really enjoyed about the game was the suspense—who would turn first; how close could we come without colliding. But all that was removed when you played with Peter. He never veered away, and not because he was any braver than the rest of us; he just seemed to enjoy the crash. It took all the suspense away for me and led me to believe that perhaps insanity ran in his family. Once, he even suggested we try it against a car.

"You are a chicken," he said.

"Yeah, and you're nuts. I'm going to Clark Street."

I grabbed the rope to my sled and started off.

"It's too damn far," he said. "Besides, you said your dad was gonna give us a ride."

"Well, he's not here, is he?"

I kept moving, listening over my shoulder for the sound of his boots. I got about twenty yards away and was just about to give in when he called out.

"Okay, damn it, I'll go. You always get your way."

It was about a mile walk to Clark Street, but you could save a couple of blocks by cutting through behind St. Anthony's. Being winter, the grounds were pretty empty, but during the summer there would always be a group of boys hanging around back of the church, playing basketball or marbles, or just trading baseball cards. When Frank was still an altar boy we would sometimes go early, before church, and sit and feed the pigeons, Frank in his black and white and me in my Sunday best. One of the kids had referred to him as St. Francis, but Frank quickly put an end to that. It was back there where he caught his first pigeon, a beautiful white female.

In fact, it was an incident involving a pigeon that had ended his career as an altar boy. Frank was twelve at the time. We no longer went to school there but we were still obliged to show up for services on Sunday (the last remnant of "the deal").

We were waiting for Father Steven to unlock the back door—Frank had on his gown and I wore my brown suit (the sleeves of which now fell about an inch above my wrists), a plain blue tie knotted in a single Windsor (a knot formed once by my father a year or so before, enabling me to merely loosen the tie and pull it over my head after use; I didn't actually learn to tie one myself until years later.), a white shirt and a pair of black shoes freshly polished and one size too small—when Rick Thornton showed up with a buddy of his. Rick was a couple of years older than Frank, big for his age and mean. His father abandoned Rick and his mother when Rick was ten. Rick's brother (Father Steven) had stepped in to help fill the void, setting about from day one to create a replica of himself, forcing Rick to be an altar boy, cramming religion down his throat, which only seemed to make Rick that much meaner.

Rick always wore a heavy leather jacket and engineer boots, even in summer. As he spoke he persistently popped his gum.

"Whatcha doin' Frankie?"

"Waiting for your brother to open the door. And my name's Frank, not Frankie."

He looked at me. "Hey, squirt. You know what shit sounds like when it hits the wall? Wop!"

Rick and his friend both laughed. Frank and I had heard that line so many times it could no longer conjure up the slightest bit of provocation. We had come to learn the best way to deal with those remarks and with Rick Thornton in general, was to ignore them. Of course, Rick was not one to be ignored. It was like something was eating at him all the time and the only way he could keep it out of his mind was to stir up the water around him.

He started in on me, fooling with my tie, trying to smudge my freshly polished shoes, but was shortly distracted by a light scraping sound coming from within one of the trash-cans. He walked over to it and brushed aside a few scraps of paper.

"Well, whadaya know; look what I found."

He reached into the can and retrieved a small brown pigeon. It had white and black specks on its chest. One of its wings was slightly mangled and one of its legs just dangled freely, obviously broken.

Rick held it out in front of him, his hands cupped like a priest serving communion, the frightened bird softly cooing as it nervously darted its head.

"Cute little bugger, ain't it," said Rick.

"Can I see it?" asked Frank.

"What for?"

"Maybe I could fix its leg. I've got some pigeons at home. I could put him in with them."

———

Frank had built a coop in our back yard and started collecting them—despite my father's objections—and before we knew, he had over twenty birds. Neighborhood cats would linger close by, licking their chops. Frank and I would toss rocks at them or press Kelly (our dog) into action, but minutes later they would return, patiently awaiting their big opportunity—an unlocked door, a back turned a minute too long. My father would arrive home from work only to be greeted by the sight of half a dozen cats perched atop the nursery cleaning themselves or catching a little afternoon sun. At night they would rattle the cages and work the birds into a frenzy. This went on for a full year—more pigeons, more cats, more cages and droppings. My father kept threatening to get rid of them and he and Frank fought constantly about it, until finally nature stepped in and wiped out three fourths of them with a virus. Frank let the rest go, hoping they might not get contaminated. The cages sat empty for another six months until one afternoon my father tore the whole thing down.

———

Frank reached for the pigeon but Rick pushed him away. "Not so quick, runt. Maybe I wanna start my own collection."

"Awh, give him the damn bird," said his friend.

Rick turned on his friend.

"Butt out, asshole."

A light went on inside the office in the back of the church. Outside the gate we could hear the people as they arrived for the service. The ten forty-five bells began to ring. Rick turned his head briefly toward the steeple and then, without any warning, grabbed the bird around the neck and gave it a quick spin in the air, snapping its neck. He then casually flipped it onto the ground and wiped his hands on his pants. Frank and I were stunned. Even Rick's friend was confounded. He stood with his mouth agape, shaking his head. Rick turned to him.

"You got a problem?"

"No, Rick, I just..."

"Good. Close your mouth before you catch something. Just a dumb pigeon. Leg was broke anyway. I did it a favor"

He started toward the back door to the church. "Time to get holy, Frankie."

The three of us stood motionless for a few seconds and then Frank bent over and picked up the pigeon. Tears filled his eyes. The sound of the door closing behind Rick reverberated across the courtyard like a gunshot. Frank held the bird to his chest, gently stroking its back, tiny drops of blood dripping over his fingers. After a minute or so, he walked over to the trashcan and gently laid the bird atop it, and without so much as a glance toward Rick's friend, or me, he beat a deliberate path to the door. I followed him in.

Inside, Rick had begun attending the altar, his boots and jacket replaced by the soft slippers and flowing black robe. Father Steven thumbed through his bible, placing an occasional marker in the appropriate sections. A handful of people had entered the church. Frank grabbed an empty chalice and moved toward Rick.

"You're late," said Father Steven, catching a glimpse of Frank out of the corner of his eye. At the sound of his voice, Rick spun around just in time to receive a glancing blow as Frank brought the chalice to his head. Rick screamed and fell to the floor, grabbing his head in pain, and Frank kicked him in the gut.

He was about to kick him again when Father Steven grabbed him by the hair and yanked him away.

"This is a house of God!"

Blood trickled from Rick's wound. Frank managed to land a kick to the priest's shin and he released his hair, whereby Frank immediately went after Rick again, landing another kick to his chest.

Father Steven limped over to the two boys, his anger exacerbated by the pain in his knee, grabbed Frank by one shoulder, spun him around and slapped him hard across the face.

"Get out of my church," he said. Frank stood silent for a few seconds then glared down at Rick, who grinned back.

"Out!" repeated the priest.

"It's not yours," said Frank, who then dropped the chalice at Father Steven's feet, turned and left the church. I followed. Outside, he stopped and picked up the bird, tucked it into his jacket and carried it home.

———

It being Sunday and church about to start made me a little hesitant to take the shortcut, but Peter insisted. We were almost through the grounds when Father Philip came out of the Rectory, headed toward the church. When he saw us he made the slight detour and cut across our path.

"Oh, great," I said.

"Good morning, boys."

"Morning Father," I said.

Father Philip was a huge man, mostly bald, a hard, chiseled face, and a real penchant for cigars and cussing. My parents had pulled us all out of the Catholic school when I was eight, but during my three years there, I had grown to both fear and like the man. Between the enigma of Heaven and the iniquity of Hell stood Father Philip.

"Where you boys off to today?"

"Clark Street." I said.

"Haven't seen you in church lately, Michael."

"No Father, I, uh, well, I was kind of sick last week and the week before that I..."

"Don't let the Devil catch you with a mortal sin on your soul," he said. Then he smiled and added. "If you don't make it to church, at least come to confession—cover yourself."

"Yes, Father, I will. I'll come next week."

"Good. And bring your brother. Peter, how's your father?"

Peter shrugged his shoulders. "I don't know. Okay, I guess."

"I'll be sure and say a prayer for him. Well, you boys have a good time today." He hurried off to the church and we continued on our way.

"Boy," said Peter, "you still believe all that crap about hell?"

"I believe in God," I said, as if saying it aloud would reaffirm my conviction. I watched closely for Peter's response.

"I'm an atheist," he said, undoubtedly another one of his father's secret words.

"What's that?"

"Somebody who doesn't believe in God."

"You'll go to hell if you don't believe in God."

"If there's no God, then there's no Devil, either. So I can't go to hell."

Peter's brother, Pat, was the only McBride who still went to church, who had any religious life at all, but I had never heard Peter say that (deny God's existence) before. In fact, though I had heard there were people without belief, I had never, until that moment, heard it spoken. (Even Frank, who stopped going to church after his confrontation with Father Steven, never went so far as to suggest there was no God.) Peter's words seemed foreign, unattached to any sense of reality I had ever known, and made me fear for him. I changed the subject.

"You tell Mary you could go all the way around on the swing?"

Peter grinned his toothless grin. "Your sister sure is dumb."

"She didn't believe you," I said, not so much to defend her but to thwart his feeling of superiority.

"She did too!"

"Did not! Do you have to keep whistling all the time? You sound like a dumb teapot or something."

"Yeah, you wanna do something about it."

"Sounds dumb," I said.

"I can't help it."

There was a bit of mystery surrounding Peter's missing teeth. Mrs. Grady claimed there was a fight at the McBride house that night and that Mr. McBride had knocked them out, and although she was the town gossip and mostly ignored, most everyone on the block believed her this time; nobody liked McBride and it suited them well to have him be the villain. Peter claimed he fell getting out of his bed, the upper half of a bunk bed, and hit his mouth on the corner of his dresser. His brother, Pat, played dumb, claiming he had slept through the whole thing. The neighborhood was slightly disturbed over the whole incident for a few days but then quickly settled down to the status quo, as though a small tremor had passed underfoot, just enough to register on the scale but not enough to tumble any structures.

"Look," I said, "they've got the saw-horses up," and Peter and I ran the remaining fifty yards to the corner where a half dozen boys gathered about.

Clark Street ran level, north and south, the whole distance of our small town, until it reached Spring Street, where it dipped radically for two blocks behind St. Mary's Hospital. When it iced over it was impossible to negotiate in a car, so every winter the blockades were put up, sometimes for as long as a month straight.

We would gather at the top of the steep street, divide into teams and race to the bottom, or we would free-for-all, tackling one another as we went, sending an unmanned sled speeding recklessly downward, smacking the head of a fallen warrior further below or just sliding unencumbered all the way to the bottom and part way up the other side until gravity finally sucked it down.

That morning the hill looked perfect. The fresh snow had provided a cushion over the hard ice, which allowed for quick runs with less chance of cracking open one's skull. The close proximity of the hospital had been advantageous on more than one occasion. Fingers had been sliced open from the sharp runners, noses broken, wrists sprained. There had even been a concussion. Fortunately for us, it had obviously never occurred to anyone that perhaps they should keep us kids from sledding down the street.

My mother's job as a cook at St. Mary's worked out great for me. Peter and I would often stop in for lunch, saving us the long trek back home. She had been off the previous month because of Martin but if Rose was cooking there was a strong possibility of a free meal.

Someone in the crowd yelled "free-for-all" and we quickly herded together, jockeying for position, securing our hats and gloves, bragging about how we were each going to be the first to reach the bottom. As I pulled my hat over my ears, I glanced toward the hospital where some of the patients had propped themselves up in their beds to catch a glimpse of the action, their tired arms waving, slowly, methodically across the face of the pitted glass. I waved indiscriminately toward them.

On the ground floor, in the far window, there was something new; an object being casually waved back and forth, as if the person holding it had spotted someone he knew. It looked like a hat of some sort. A yellow hat. I glanced around at the other kids, but none of them seemed to notice it. I waved back and the hat came to a rest.

"Everybody ready?" a voice called out.

"No crashing into someone after they fall," came another voice and someone else yelled "sissy," and we were off, a dozen boys in search of a small portion of glory.

Peter got hit early, his sled flying out from under him and continuing on half way down the hill. He cursed as he jumped to his feet and I set out after the boy who had hit him.

My sled is fast and I soon catch up to the culprit, sliding up directly behind him, an occasional fan of snow slapping across my face. I grab his foot and give it a little shake and he turns his head to see me, panic in his eyes, a large grin on my face. He tries to shake me off, a sharp turn to the left, another to the right, but I hold steady as we increase our speed down the steep hill. Finally, I make my move, angling my sled to the left to go around him, still holding on to his foot. His sled begins to dig a runner and slow down, and as I overtake him, I spin him in a semi-circle, releasing him as I pass, his sled toppling over half a dozen times, the boy sprawled out face first in the snow.

I am in heaven.

———

We went on for hours, till most of us were soaked through to the bone, our fingers and toes stiffening, our bodies weak from the repetitive climb up the hill. Each time I reached the top I'd see the yellow hat waving to me and I'd wave back.

"I'm freezing," said Peter.

"Let's go over to the hospital and get something to eat."

"Naw, I better get home. Is your mom working, today?"

I stared at Peter in disbelief. "My mom just had a baby so I really doubt she'd be working today. Don't you know anything?"

"Well, I don't live there, you know."

Once again I saw the waving hat.

"Look," I said.

"What?"

"In the window. It's been there all morning."

Peter turned and looked toward the window but his mind was on the cold. "I don't see nothing."

"In the window. The hat," I said.

"So what," he said. Let's go. It's cold." He started to walk away and I went after him.

"Hey, wait up. Maybe my mom knows who it is."

"Who cares?"

"Wanna come over tonight?" I asked.

"What for?"

"We got a new Sears catalogue. We could look at stuff."

"Uh, I don't know. Could I see the baby?"

"I guess...if you want. It's kind of ugly, though."

"I don't know. I'm probably gonna be in trouble when I get home."

I turned for one last look at the window but the hat had disappeared behind the lowered shade, closed off now like all the other windows across the face of the building, like so many tired eyes resigned to sleep. A quiet fell over the street as all the boys retreated in their separate directions, the ruts gouged out by our runners the only sign of our having been there. If it snowed hard enough tonight, even they would disappear. Somewhere behind the thick curtain of clouds the sun slowly dropped. It seemed a shame to leave while there was still daylight but I could no longer feel my toes.

FOUR

I was starving after such a long day on the hill and wasted no time in devouring my dinner. (I even finished my vegetables.) My father was working late again; a young couple had fallen asleep on the train and missed their stop so he got the call to run them up to Peoria. Nobody liked those long runs, for by the time the customer paid his fare he would have little left for a tip. There was, however, one occasion when my father took some high roller all the way to Chicago (a hundred miles) in the middle of winter. A gambler who'd hit it big on the numbers, the man was afraid somebody would rob him on the train. He gave my father a fifty-dollar tip—up front—to take him to pick up his winnings and safely deliver him back to our little town. It was exceptionally cold that night with spots of black ice along the highway. It took him six hours to make the roundtrip, but he was whistling when he came in from that particular run.

My mother rocked Martin in the bassinet with one hand while she ate with the other, all the time staring across the room as if she could see through the wall. Carol had gone to watch Richard (her boyfriend) play basketball, and the rest of us were just finishing up our meal.

"Do we have anything for dessert?" I asked.

My mother continued to rock the baby, seemingly oblivious to my question. Mary looked at me and shrugged.

"Mom."

"I can bake some apples," she said without looking up.

"Cooking an apple doesn't exactly turn it into dessert," said Frank.

"Don't we have any ice cream?" asked Mary.

Finally my mother looked up from her plate. She smiled. "No, we don't, but if Frank wants to run across the street and get some, I'll give him the money."

All eyes on Frank.

"I'm gonna go check on Kelly," he said.

"I'll go get it," I said.

"Bring me my purse. I think it's on the couch."

"Can I go downstairs with Frank?" asked Mary.

"No, you can't," said Frank.

"Why not? Mom."

My mother turned to Frank. "Why can't she come?"

"Because, she always wants to come."

"Mary, you help me with the dishes and when Michael gets back we'll have some ice cream?"

"But I want to go see Kelly."

Frank got up and began making his way toward the kitchen, victorious on both fronts.

"Hold it right there, young man."

Frank slowed his pace but kept moving.

"Mary, you can go down after the dishes are done. And you, be nice to your sister," she called out to Frank as he disappeared into the kitchen. "And check the furnace while you're down there."

"Yeah, sure," Frank yelled out. So he had lost a small battle. In a house full of such skirmishes, an occasional defeat was to be expected. There were no grudges held. The four of us—Anna had by now removed herself and Martin was still too young—would come up against one another's will and if we were unable to resolve the given problem, my mother would step in. (Somehow, we managed to keep our disputes to a minimum around my father.)

If the conflict involved any freedom of movement, she tended to give Frank and I more rope. We were boys, after all, and in nineteen fifty-eight, it was still a man's world—for better or for worse. So where Carol, when she was fourteen, had to be home at night by dark, it was not uncommon for Frank to show up at ten o'clock, not a word said. It was not a question of trust, but rather one of protection. Girls seemed to be more vulnerable to whatever dangers lurked out there. (There weren't many in our town.) We were expected to look out for our sisters, and to treat all girls in a gentle manner. Our roles as different sexes were well defined. The challenge to that simplistic definition would thrust our generation into a war of the sexes in the years ahead. The seeds of that war, however, were not sown in our house, or town.

I went for the ice cream.

Slovak's store was directly across from our house and in fact had been built at the same time and was almost identical to ours, two stories, brown composition shingle siding and roof, white wood windows, and a small front porch. It was like looking into a mirror every time you walked out the front door. Mr. and Mrs. Slovak lived in the rear of the building. They had added on a couple of rooms a few years back and had, it seemed to me, the perfect situation: unlimited food of all varieties right in their own home—day or night!

It was obvious from their size the Slovak's liked the idea too. Both were very fat (borderline obese) and rather slovenly but, as anyone in town would tell you, two gentler souls could not be found.

Mr. Slovak took care of the books and did all the heavy work while Mrs. Slovak worked the register. They had no children of their own so it gave her particular pleasure to wait on any of the neighborhood kids. I had just begun going in there again recently after what had happened the previous summer.

Every Sunday morning, Mr. Slovak would don his brown suit and plain black tie, while Mrs. Slovak squeezed into one of three floral print dresses (she rotated them), and splash about a quart of perfume over her large neck and arms. If the wind was blowing just right, you could smell the aroma in our back yard. The two of them would then walk arm in arm to St. Anthony's for mass. Mr. Slovak had a swift gait but on these mornings he would slow down to accommodate his wife's more relaxed pace—what Frank referred to as her waddle. They would leave their house at precisely 10:45 (uncharacteristically prompt—you could set your watch by their departure), make the fifteen minute walk to St. Anthony's, spend an hour in church, socialize for fifteen minutes or so on the church steps after the service, and then make the somewhat laborious walk back home, arriving around twelve thirty.

We liked the Slovaks, and it was not our intention to rob them, but living so close and seeing all those great treats day after day—m & ms, milk duds, ice cream sandwiches, popsicles, rolls and rolls of dot candies!—well, it was just too much.

So, one Sunday morning, as the huge couple made the turn at the corner and disappeared from sight of the store, we made our move. George Price, who lived next door to the store, hoisted his little brother, Tom, through an open window in back, and he then let the rest of us in through the side door. Frank didn't want Tom to come with us; he was only nine and, Frank felt, untrustworthy.

Once inside, of course, we were immediately bombarded with the aromatic trail of Mrs. Slovack's pungent perfume, an assault so bad that Frank actually stood at the back door fanning the room with the door, risking our detection to the neighbors in the process. After a few minutes the odor seemed to diminish—or we just got used to it—and we proceeded to gorge ourselves. Frank made himself a banana split using three different flavors, topped it with whipped cream and a half a dozen cherries and sprinkled it with a handful of nuts. Tom and I started out with candy bars, a Butterfinger dipped in vanilla ice cream for me, and a Three Musketeers for him. George made himself a ham and cheese sandwich, claiming he hadn't had his breakfast and didn't want to fill up on junk. To wash it all down we invaded the sodas, which were kept in a cooler, the bottles suspended by their necks in a metal rack. In order to free the bottle from the rack you had to put in a nickel and slide it to the end of the rack and up through the release valve. We simply popped the caps off with an opener and inserted straws into the bottles.

It went on for close to an hour, till all of us were feeling stuffed and somewhat sick. We each filled our pockets with penny candies and bubble-gum, and Tom wrapped a sheet of dot-candies around his waist like a belt of ammunition, then we quickly cleaned up our mess, covering our tracks as best as possible.

We were about to leave when I spotted something I just had to have. Mrs. Slovak had hung a curtain in the doorway separating the store from their living area. On a shelf adjacent to the curtain—just out of my reach—was a jar filled with licorice sticks. Frank said to leave it, that we'd had enough. But I couldn't let it go. I climbed up on a chair to get to them but as I grabbed the jar, the chair slipped out from under me. My natural instinct was to grab hold of something to break my fall; I chose the curtain, ripping it off the rod as I fell to the ground. I landed hard on my back, still clutching the jar of licorice, the torn curtain draped over my aching body.

"Jesus!" said Frank. "Now you've done it."

We tried in vain to repair the damage, but time was against us. It was already past twelve. I looked to Frank. "What are we gonna do?"

"Stay here. I'll be right back." Frank ran across the street and returned shortly with Mary—her sewing kit in hand—thinking a woman's touch was what we needed. When Mary realized what we had been up to, she just shook her head. "Dad's gonna kill you guys when he finds out."

"Can you fix it?" asked Frank.

"Oh, now you want me around, huh?"

"Come on Mary, please." I said.

"You can go to the movies with us this Saturday," said Frank.

"Every Saturday," said Mary.

"Every Saturday! No way," said Frank.

"Suit yourself," said Mary and she started walking toward the door.

Frank and I looked at each other. "Every other Saturday for the next two months," said Frank.

"Three months," said Mary, "and you pay my way."

It was a deal. In no time at all Mary had the seam sewn and the curtain tacked back up as best she could; we placed the licorice jar back on the shelf and left. Maybe, we thought, they won't notice.

I stayed away from the store the entire next week. Each morning as I left for school I would glance over there expecting to see Mr. or Mrs. Slovak giving me the evil eye, but nothing happened.

Once a week my mother would give us each a nickel for a treat, but when she offered it up on Wednesday I refused it, saying my stomach didn't feel quite right. "What about you, Mary?" she said. Mary glanced over at me and very casually answered. "No, maybe later." My mother sensed something was up but she didn't push it.

That Saturday, Carol and Richard offered to take me to a movie. As we left the house I could see Mr. Slovak sitting by the side door to his house, his back against the wall, the small chair completely enveloped by his rotund body as he gently rocked on the two hind legs; he appeared to levitate. He stared over at us. I tried to look away but for some reason I kept returning to his stare. It was as if he were leaving it up to me. I know what you did, his eyes were saying. Now what are you going to do about it?

Carol and Richard started across the street; it was our custom to cut through the Slovak's yard to the alley behind their house when going to town.

"Let's go this way," I said, pointing up our street.

"What for?" said Richard.

"I don't know. I just don't want to go that way." Guilt flooded my face.

"What's the matter, Michael? What did you do?" said Carol.

We started across the street. "Nothing. I just don't want to go this way."

As we were passing Mr. Slovak, I kept my head down.

"Good morning, Mr. Slovak," said Carol.

"Morning. Where you kids off to?"

"Taking this juvenile delinquent to the movies," said Richard, having no idea how accurate his description of me was. They stopped. I tried not to look up but once again I could feel the pull of Mr. Slovak's eyes and when at last I braved a peek he was staring right at me.

But there was no malice in that look. Mr. Slovak always had a bit of a twinkle in his eye, as though he were about to tell you a funny story, or like he had the inside scoop on life and found it all so ironic.

"How's that knee of yours doing, Richard?"

"Doctor says it should be better by the time the season starts. I hope so."

"Well, good luck with it," he said, still staring at me. We started away again. I was beginning to feel like I'd made it, that I had negotiated the minefield and was about to pass into the friendly territory, when he called out to me.

"Michael, can I speak to you for a minute?"

"Well, we're going to a movie right now..."

"This'll just take a minute. You can catch up."

"Okay. Sure."

Carol and Richard continued on toward town. I was grateful for that.

"You want to tell me about Sunday?"

I shifted about nervously. "Uh, what do you mean?"

He smiled. "Well, I spoke to Mrs. Price yesterday, and I was curious what you might have to tell me."

Tom had panicked and told his parents what happened. George had forced him to climb through the rear window because he was the only one small enough to fit. Of course, he tried to talk us out of it but we wouldn't listen. I explained to Mr. Slovak that we were only looking around and that we didn't mean to rip the curtain. We were, after all, only kids. He placed both hands on his belly, as if this would put him more in touch with the demons that drove us to raid his cache of goods.

"I'm disappointed in you boys," he said. "How am I going to be able to trust you in the future?"

"Oh, you can," I said. "We won't do it again, I promise."

"Uh, huh. What do you think your parents will say when they find out?"

I pleaded with him not to tell my parents. Maybe he'd seen my father chasing Frank down the street a few times, heard the profanities, understood the situation, or maybe, not having children of his own, he was more sympathetic. Whatever the reason, he agreed not to tell them, but he wanted a list of everything we ate—an accurate one—so that he could arrive at the cost. And he wanted Frank to come over and talk to him.

"Oh, by the way," he said. "Tell Mary, Mrs. Slovak says if she wants to make a little extra money, she can help her with some sewing. Now, one last thing: You understand, don't you, that what you did was wrong?"

"Yes, sir," I said. I felt embarrassed and ashamed.

"Good. Listen. You didn't kill anybody, but there is such a thing as right and wrong in this world. It's best to learn that over something as simple as this. The principle is the important thing here. You understand what I'm trying to say?"

"Yes, sir. I think so."

"Okay, enough said. Now, go enjoy your movie," he added and I beat it out of there.

That night, I told Frank what happened and he said he'd go over and speak to Mr. Slovak. I told him I was going to let

Tom have it for squealing but Frank said I would look a little silly picking on a nine-year-old. "Besides," he said, "Thornton will probably work his way down to him eventually."

So, we were feeling okay. We'd been caught and it was embarrassing facing Mr. Slovak, but our parents hadn't found out. And the money...well, that part might be tough but we'd find a way.

Then the phone rang. My father answered it. We could hear his voice, very steady, but we couldn't make out what he was saying. The conversation was brief. I didn't give it much thought until I heard his footsteps coming up the stairs, very deliberate and steady, like his voice. We waited quietly in anticipation. He arrived and spoke only to Frank.

"What the hell are you trying to do!" The control he had displayed over the phone had vanished.

"Ain't trying to do nothing."

"You call breaking into our neighbors house, nothing?"

"We didn't break in," said Frank.

I tried telling him it was my idea to sneak into the house, that we had already worked things out with Mr. Slovak, but he didn't want to hear it. "What do you take me for, some kind of jack-ass?"

This was a crucial point. Up to now my father had been yelling, had been trying to establish his position as the power in our house. Had Frank been humble and apologetic, had he recognized my father's authority, there would have been some more yelling, perhaps a warning, a few more profanities, and then things would have cooled down. But Frank was not one to back down.

"How many kinds are there?" he said, very cool and ironic.

With this my father moved in real close to Frank—who

was still sitting on the bed—and doubled up his fist.

"You son-of-bitch, you don't talk to me that way!"

"I'll talk to you any way I want." Frank remained collected. My mother reached the top of the steps, Mary close behind.

"You think you're ready for me you little bastard!"

"Sam, please. Frank, your sister."

There was a pause in the action. Mary held on to my mother's leg. My father's whole body was taut. An immigrant's son, he had learned to fight at any early age, defending his Italian heritage, and had even done well as a boxer in the Golden Gloves. Uneducated, unskilled, knocked down by life, he now stood poised over his teenaged son, defending what little pride he had left.

Frank got up from his bed and pushed his way by us all and started down the stairs. "Tell that asshole to get off my back," he said and my father chased him out of the house.

I don't know who told my father but I don't believe it was Mr. Slovak. Frank spent the night at a friend's house and the next day he and I made up the list which he took over to the Slovaks. They say Italians don't hold their feelings in, that we're healthier for it. We scream and yell and then make up and all is well. That's easy to say if you don't live with it. There was the screaming and the yelling, but there was no making up, just a gradual chipping away at the grit that connects a father to a son until eventually they just fall away from one another.

———

Mildew permeated our cellar, even in the summer. We had an old ringer washer set up in a little alcove and in the winter the clothes were hung to dry throughout most of the cellar, the lines criss-crossing the rooms so when the clothes were hung, a maze of sorts was created. In the very back of the cellar, which was at the front of the house, was the furnace (that sounds contradictory, but because of the layout— the largest room being under the kitchen—going to the furnace area always seemed like going deeper into the house) and off to one side, a small coal bin. Next to the furnace, on a small piece of carpet, lay Kelly, a black female mutt, very much pregnant. Frank was sitting next to her when I arrived.

"Hey, girl. I put my hand to her belly. "I'll bet she's going to have a lot."

"Yeah, I hope so," said Frank, as he got up and opened the door to the furnace.

"Fire's pretty low," he said and gazed down at me.

"Don't look at me. I'm not going in there."

"What's the matter, afraid of the dark?"

He picked up the shovel and I followed him as far as the entry to the bin, a small room maybe ten feet square with an opening on the outside wall covered by a piece of tin about two feet wide. Once a month the truck would arrive and the man would run the metal tube from his truck through the hole in the wall, delivering the black chunks of coal to the bin.

Frank pulled the string and turned on the light. Spiders darted into the corners, well camouflaged by the pitch-black chunks of coal. He was the only one other than my father who would come down to the cellar alone to fuel the furnace. In fact, he would stay down there for hours just talking to Kelly or shooting the BB gun. Once he shot me in the arm by accident. It stung like hell but I was the center of attention at school for a few days.

"Someone could climb right through that hole if they wanted to," I said.

"Who would want to do that?"

"I don't know. A burglar."

"That's a joke. What are they gonna steal, the clothes line?"

He filled the shovel and delivered his load to the furnace, then returned for another.

"Just think," I said, "if you were Superman, you could crush some of that coal into diamonds."

"Yeah, right. Turn off the light," he said and I quickly stepped into the bin, pulled the string and jumped back out. He tossed the second load of coal into the furnace and we both stood quietly watching the flames grow. It all seemed to have such order, such definition.

The funny thing is, I don't recall ever actually seeing anyone start the fire in the furnace. For all I knew, it was always there, like the sky or the birds or any other part of my life up till then. The man came in the truck and filled the bin with coal; the coal went into the furnace and burned, sending the heat upward into the house.

"Wanna catch some for me?"

Frank closed the furnace door. "Where?"

"We could take down the clothes"

"You guys." It was Mary. Frank looked at me mischievously.

"We're back here," he said.

Mary arrived through the maze of clothes. She had put a jacket on to come down to the cellar.

"Hi, Kelly," she said and bent down to give the dog a hug. "Don't you guys want any ice cream?"

"Maybe later," said Frank. "We were gonna play catch. You wanna play?"

"Sure!" she said, surprised at the offer.

"Okay. Why don't you take down the clothes and fold them while Mike goes upstairs and gets a ball and glove."

"They're still wet," said Mary.

"Well, then, don't fold them. Just hang them back up when we're done."

"What are you going to do?" she said.

"I'll hold the basket."

FIVE

Plumb school was a three-story brick building with a fire escape running down one side onto the asphalt playground. Originally a hotel, it had gone under after the new highway was built in fifty-one, re-routing traffic away from our small town. Up to this point, Hardscrabble was considered a thriving little city, tripling in population from five thousand to sixteen thousand in just eight years. We had a canning factory, the second largest glass company in the state, three movie theatres and from what I have been told, close to one hundred per cent employment. All that changed when we were bypassed by the highway committee, a decision made, according to my father, late at night in a smokey room with a lot of money changing hands. It was, for all intent and purposes, the death knell for Hardscrabble.

There were grades K through six at our school. I had gone to Kindergarten there and then left for three years to go to St. Anthony's. My father was somewhat of a practicing Catholic but my mother had little if any interest in religion. The "deal", as Frank referred to it, carved out more than twenty years earlier, went like this: In order for my parents to be married in the Catholic church—a must in my father's family—all the boys had to be named after saints, and all the children raised as Catholics, an unpleasant condition to which my mother finally acquiesced—that is until the uniforms came along; we simply could not afford them, and in our house the truth was, economics trumped religion.

After third grade I switched to Plumb, where the only mention of God was in the daily Pledge of Allegiance, where most of the kids were as poor or poorer than us and where even a few Negroes dotted the rooms.

In good weather we played outdoors at recess and lunch. We had a game much like baseball only we used a large rubber ball the size of a volleyball and we hit it with our fist. If you hit the ball between the second and third levels of the fire escape it was an automatic double. If you hit it over the top, it was a home run. There were only a handful of boys who could hit it over the top. Somehow, despite my size, I was one of that handful. It angered some of the bigger boys who could not quite coordinate their strength with their aim, resulting in a blistering shot just inches foul or another bouncing off the fire-escape. I don't know if I was over compensating for being little or if perhaps my timing was just a bit better, but I consistently terrorized the opposing team with my prowess.

In the winter we stayed indoors and played a game called murder, wherein we took the same balls, divided the class into two, lined up against opposite walls in the makeshift gymnasium (a large room on the ground floor that doubled for civic meetings) and set about hurling the balls across the room at one another. You could run up to the center of the room before you tossed the ball, but of course that left you vulnerable to the other team's attack. (A common sight was that of a lone invader, having released his ball, attempting to scramble back to the wall as a half dozen opponents pelted him from behind.)

To win the game, one simply had to be the last person

standing. There was nothing worse than being hit early, for it meant sitting down on the sidelines for ten to fifteen minutes, waiting for the game to end. Some of the guys who couldn't hit the ball over the fire escape saw this as an opportunity to get even with those of us who could. Two of them would approach the centerline together, pick one of us out as their intended victim and then release the balls with all their strength. Unfortunately (for them) their lack of coordination extended into the winter months, as well, for they rarely hit their target. (They did, however, manage on occasion to catch some unsuspecting girl with a couple of painful blows to the side of the head. When one girl was upended by a hit at the back of the legs and smacked down hard on her back it was decided that the girls would no longer be required to participate.)

I was a good student, straight A's every semester (of course, all of this would change later), and this presented certain advantages, like being a crosswalk guard, a position of high standing (especially with the girls), which allowed me to leave class five minutes early every day. On the downside, whenever I had P.E. for last period, I would have to leave in the middle of a game and take my position on the corner, or if I had morning duties I had to get up a few minutes earlier. Nonetheless, I wore my white belt with pride and never lost a student.

Because of my math ability (or so I was told) I got to miss half a day one year to help our principal, Mr. Barnes, work on some census thing. A short, stocky man with eyes hidden behind fatty lids, he enjoyed reciting clever little tricks like how to remember the difference between principle and principal. "Just remember," he said, "your principal is your pal."

I remember that day in his office, along with two other

students adding up numbers on stacks of paper. I would count ahead five or six sheets as fast as I could, and then turn my attention briefly to a Life Magazine I had brought along to the room. I liked reading the short pieces in Ripley's Believe It Or Not, with headlines like: High Speed Fruit Sorter Is Gentle As Human Hands; Newest Electric Refrigerator Never Runs Out Of Ice; Rocket Power, Miles Underground, Cracks Open New Pools of Oil. The articles were short and each was accompanied by a drawing. Some of them made me feel a little uneasy. The world, it seemed to me, was getting awfully complex—computers in the home, super sonic jets, men on the moon. Life seemed complicated enough to me already. I wanted things to stay the way they were.

And there was an advertisement inviting people to move to sunny California. A man in the foreground, dressed in overalls and a short sleeve shirt, held a box of oranges, and behind him were rows of trees covered with more oranges, and further in the distance, snow-capped mountains merged with a pale blue sky. It was adds like these that had caught my mother's eye. (There was talk of our moving.) I showed the picture to Mr. Barnes and expressed my concerns about whether or not school would be more difficult there and what if I was to flunk. He laughed and said he could hardly imagine me ever flunking in school, especially not in California, where scholastic levels were reportedly way below those of the mid-west.

Now, I remember the report cards, my crosswalk belt, the free six-packs of coca-cola for the good grades, but I don't remember the actual schoolwork. It's as though the lessons learned from my books were a separate reality altogether from those of my life, a lesser reality. Like a squirrel, I became a gatherer, skipping along the surface of education, collecting little tidbits of information to store away for the years to come. Tucked away in my nest were dates and names and plenty of numbers, but nothing to hold them altogether, to give them any significance.

I try to picture myself with a book in class or at home, but nothing appears. I only see the people, the events surrounding my days in class. Once, while still at St. Anthony's, I arrived late to school. Our first hour every morning was spent in church, so I had to enter after everyone was seated. I walked down the aisle until I reached one row behind Sister Mary Elizabeth, then got down on my knees and crawled to my pew in hopes of not being discovered. Upon reaching the middle of the pew I slowly slid into my seat and ever so gradually eased myself up, thinking perhaps she wouldn't notice.

At the end of his sermon Father Steven turned to retrieve the paten from the tabernacle. As others squeezed by me to exit our pew, I felt a strong hand yank at the back of my collar. It was Sister Mary Elizabeth. She pulled me upright out of my seat, dragged me into the aisle and ushered me to the rear of the church, depositing me at last in the very back pew, not a word spoken. I suppose if I had entered the church when everyone was getting up to receive communion, I might have slipped in unnoticed, but I hadn't been to church the previous Sunday, nor subsequently to confession, thereby making me the bearer of a mortal sin and ineligible to receive the body of Christ. Point is, I have no recollection of the content of the mass that day.

————

There was not enough time before dark to go to Clark Street after school, so on these days I would keep busy in the back yard practicing my pitching. I would build a snow-man early in the season and use his head as a target. On a good afternoon it was not unusual to go through two or three heads. Or I would work on a snow fort in preparation for one of our weekend wars. In my fort I would dig out a series of holding areas and fill them up with snowballs. Some would have chutes through which I would load the snow-balls. The first of these chutes, a vertical cylinder two feet long, proved a failure for some of the snowballs broke up upon landing. But with constant revision I finally arrived at a system of curves and angles that delivered the ammunition completely intact. I was ready for battle.

———

Half a dozen boys divide into teams and begin barraging one another with snowballs. A few minutes into the action Frank, and John Mituzak show up and begin pelting both teams. I duck, along with Peter, behind my fort, where an ample supply of munitions awaits. Peter sticks his head up and catches a shot in the chin. "Ouch!" He ducks back down, his pride hurt more than his face. I spot Frank approaching us on our left flank. I nudge Peter. "On three," I say. "One, two, three!" We both stand and deliver our load—two direct hits. Frank attempts to return our volley but from behind him comes another blast, this one from Carol's boyfriend, Richard, who has shown up with two of his friends and joined in the battle. Peter and I again rise and fire but this time at Richard. Peter catches him square in the face and Richard attacks our fort, throwing himself into the wall and breaking it down with his weight. We have just enough time to blast him again before he rises to his feet. Our fort is destroyed, but we escape.

On Wednesday, a new storm came in, a warm one, bringing rain and driving me indoors after school.

On days like this I stayed upstairs until dinner. I had a collection of bottle caps and would divide them into armies (Pepsi Cola vs. a pieced together army of Dad's Root beer, Orange Nesbitt and 7Up) and do battle, or I'd break out my baseball cards. I had shoeboxes full of every card imaginable, current and old, and had even created a game wherein I would set the players out in their respective positions in the field and then draw cards from a pile of three-by-fives-cut in half-to determine the action. At first the game was rather raw and unrealistic but eventually I was able to refine it to a credible likeness of the real thing with records for each team and individual players.

It was the '58 season that had prompted the invention. It had been a bad year. The Dodgers, playing their first season in L.A. had dropped from a respectable third place in '57, to seventh in '58, beating out only the lowly Phillies. I had a small transistor radio and listened to every game, coaxing them on, believing faith alone could bring them success. But it became apparent by mid season that they were going nowhere but down. And of course, everyone had a theory as to why they fell so low: the move had broken their spirit; the "wall" in left field at the Coliseum had hurt their left handed pitchers (It was a short 250 feet away.); they had lost Roy Campanella, a great catcher crippled in a car accident. I suppose there was a little truth in all of it, but for me, it was just a bad year, full of bad luck.

And so I decided to make things right. I picked four teams from the American League and four from the National. I took the top four from the American: New York, Chicago, Boston, and Cleveland. From the National I picked the top three: Milwaukee, Pittsburgh, San Francisco, and added the Dodgers. I kept Campanella and Reese in the line-up, thinking somehow the magic of Brooklyn would rub off on my team. Each team played forty-eight games—sixteen against each team in their League.

I had to make box score forms for each game by longhand. I had considered charting each player's progress on a daily basis so as to keep track of slumps and streaks but I could see myself headed for an endless pile of paper work and opted instead for a good eraser and updating batting averages and pitching percentages every five or six games.

The season progressed beautifully. The Dodgers got off to a slow start, but by the end of their twentieth game, they were in first place by two—a lead they never surrendered— and by the end of my season, it was they and the Yankees squared off to meet in the World Series. (I had cut the American league short at thirty games. The Yankees were out by five and I had already played out all the National League games. My interest was waning.)

Did I ever cheat? On occasion I would help the Dodgers along, rationalizing my intrusions whenever possible: Duke would have caught that ball, or, Drysdale would never give up that many home runs. So I would grab the offensive card and stick it in the back of the pile—it's amazing how well a player can do given a second chance—glancing over my shoulder to make sure nobody saw my little indiscretion (as if anyone cared). This was my world, and although I wanted to emulate the real one in as many ways as possible, I also wanted control. I wanted a team to come from behind on occasion. I wanted a guy in a slump to hit a game-winning home run. If that meant fudging a little, so be it.

———

I kept a close eye on the weather for I feared the ice would all melt and Clark Street would open up to traffic, but the rain only served to bring more ice as the temperature dropped each night, and then by Friday the rain turned to snow and on Saturday conditions were perfect.

SIX

When I was a boy, we rarely called one another on the telephone. This was not a case of happenstance but rather a conscious effort on our parents part to keep us off the phone. It was, in their minds, a tool to be used when needed to convey important information. The image of a teenager lying back on the couch, chatting with a friend, did not exist in our house. I had never questioned this routine but I'm sure if one of my older siblings had, they would have been greeted with my father's sole answer to the question why: "Because I said so."

My father had other pat answers too. "When you get your own house, you can stay up as late as you want. When you get your own house you can stay out after dark. When you get your own house…" And of course, his favorite one was "over my dead body." Now, I never talked back to my father when I was young (Frank was the one who covered that angle), with one exception. You would think that since it happened only once, I would recall the details, but I don't. I only know we were standing half way up the stairs, I was arguing with him about something and it was shortly after he and Frank had been fighting (so I suspect I said what I said in some kind of allegiance to Frank) when he pulled out the "over my dead body" line, to which I replied. "Yeah, well, that can be arranged." Now, here's the thing: Had

Frank used that line, my father would have chased him out of the house and down the street, but in this case he merely fell silent, turned and slowly walked down the stairs and into the other room.

I felt very clever, having come up with that line, but at the same time I felt like it wasn't really me, that I had stepped outside of myself to cut him. When my mother took me aside that night and told me I had hurt my father's feelings and that I needed to apologize, I was more than eager to comply.

So we rarely called our friends on the phone, and if we did, we kept it short. Nor were we inclined to knock on a friend's door. There was a certain formality to knocking on one's door that just never sat right with me, or any of my friends, for that matter. Our chosen procedure was to stand out front of a friend's house and call out his name, stretching the first syllable so that Peter, for example, would come out sounding like Peeeter, with the second syllable falling a minor third below the first. This, I'm pretty sure, was our own invention, borne, I have no doubt, out of our desire to circumvent formality and to minimize any contact with our friends' parents, an event always guaranteed boring at best.

I stood outside Peter's house early Saturday morning calling his name but there was no response, this despite the fact I could hear voices coming from within his house, and was pretty certain he was home. I considered knocking but it sounded like a fight going on inside, or not so much a fight but just Mr. McBride yelling, a not uncommon scenario. I tried calling out to Peter one last time and then gave up the effort and returned home to wait for Frank. He had been up late with Kelly the night before and was still asleep when I left the house. I passed the time watching television, Lash LaRue and then The Lone Ranger, until finally around ten o'clock Frank pulled himself out of bed.

It took him another hour before he was finally ready to go. It's funny, one of the few things Frank and our father had in common was their aversion to getting up early. And once out of bed, both were painfully slow at getting themselves ready for the day. Frank could spend a half an hour in the bathroom, something that I have never done once in my entire life. He set his own pace early on in life and has stuck to it. This was a constant irritation to my father who, when he told you to do something, wanted it done now, and yet, he was exactly the same way, slow, deliberate and unwilling to change his pace for anyone.

After what seemed like an eternity, Frank was finally ready and we headed out. We stopped by John Matuzak's house on the way and he went with us. John was a good-natured guy, slightly overweight yet still an excellent athlete, straight brown hair parted on the left and trimmed closely around the ears. He had large teeth and a huge smile. Everybody liked John. He was a freshman (one year older than Frank) and had already made the junior varsity basketball team. He and Frank were good friends and I liked John well enough, but having him along reduced my stature to that of the tag-along. Peter and I would often follow them whenever they would take their BB guns and go into the woods. We'd hide behind trees and toss rocks down their path, giggling with delight as they quietly approached their prey, rifles pumped and ready, signaling one another with hand gestures as they split apart to form a cross-fire. Once, when they heard us laughing, they opened fire on us, but we were out of range, a fact I'm pretty sure they were well aware of.

The new storm had brought with it an extremely cold

mass of air causing the temperature to actually drop as the day proceeded, so that by one o'clock we were well under freezing. After a few runs down the hill my toes and fingers were numb, and we were all ready to call it a day. I had forgotten about the man with the yellow hat until Frank brought it up.

"You see that?" he said, and pointed to the window. There it was again. But it was different now. The previous week, the wave was more relaxed, almost rhythmic. Now it seemed chaotic, even frantic.

"I saw him last week." I said.

"Why don't you go up there?" said Frank.

"Maybe it's somebody you know," said John, and for a moment the three of us stood entranced, staring up at the window.

"Maybe Helen knows him," said Frank, breaking the spell.

"Maybe," I said as I waved, but I had heard nothing from our mother regarding anyone we knew being in the hospital. In our absorption with the figure in the window we hadn't noticed the group of boys gathering together nearby, but as they grew louder we turned our attention toward them.

"Fight!" said John, and the three of us dropped the ropes to our sleds and ran toward the crowd. There in the middle of the circle were Rick Thornton and another boy, much smaller, going at it. The smaller boy was no match for Thornton. He flailed away aimlessly while the larger, more experienced Thornton stood back and picked his shots, landing two devastating blows to the face in a row, the first one sending the smaller boy's glasses flying, the second one drawing blood and dropping him to the ground. At this point Thornton kicked him and then dropped down on top of him, sitting on his chest, pinning his arms to the ground.

The smaller boy was in tears as Thornton toyed with him, slapping him repeatedly in the face, side to side.

"Oh, the baby's crying," said Thornton and his friend joined in on the razing. "Maybe he needs his mommy."

"You want your mommy?" said Thornton. "Baby want a bottle?" He picked up a handful of snow and rubbed it in the boys face, diluting the deep red blood to a much paler hue and smearing it all over his cheeks. He tried to force some into the boy's mouth but was unable to pry his lips apart.

While there were a few isolated yells of support for the smaller boy, most of the crowd remained neutral despite their general dislike for Thornton; no one wanted to be singled out as his next victim. Thornton began slapping the boy again, but much harder now than before. I felt a hand on my shoulder as Frank moved me aside and pushed his way into the clearing.

"That's enough, Thornton, let him up."

Thornton looked over his shoulder and saw Frank.

"Screw you!" he yelled and turned his attention back to his victim.

All eyes on Frank.

"I said, that's enough." Frank grabbed Thornton by the collar of his jacket and jerked him away from the boy. The crowd grew silent as Thornton jumped to his feet, enraged. Thornton's friend started toward Frank but John stepped between them and the boy quickly back away.

It had been two years since the incident in the church, and though I'm certain their paths had crossed many times since, Thornton had never sought revenge. Like any bully, he fed on fear. Had he come after Frank the very next day, perhaps he could have beaten him (after all, Frank had caught him off guard) but with each passing day, Frank's confidence grew stronger, as did Thornton's self-doubt. Now, two years later, Frank had put on weight and grown a good six inches, so that he was every bit as big as Thornton.

"You dick. Why don't you mind your own business?"

A couple of boys helped the injured boy to his feet while I picked up his glasses and wiped away the snow; one lens was shattered. The boy grabbed the glasses from me and ran off crying.

"What's the matter, run out of pigeons?" said Frank.

Thornton leaned into Frank's face, fists clenched, his body swelling up like an over-inflated balloon. Frank stood cool, open hands at his sides, as if maybe he was holding the pin. Thornton glanced quickly to the crowd as they waited now in quiet anticipation, then he turned back to Frank. "Just stay out of my way," he said and then walked around Frank.

"You too, punk," he said as he shoved his way past me and barreled through the parting crowd. As he melted into the driving snow the crowd returned to life, gathering around Frank, their new hero.

Frank grabbed me by the arm. "Let's go."

We went back for our sleds and the crowd slowly dispersed into small groups, anxious, no doubt, to recall the events of the fight to one another.

"That was great," I said.

"Yeah," said John. "I think he's afraid of you."

"He's just like every other bully," said Frank. "Just a coward." He turned to me. "You probably want to steer clear of him for awhile. He'll be looking for revenge and he's going to go after someone he knows he can beat."

I was fully aware that I would have no chance in a fight

with Thornton, but to hear Frank say so with such a matter of fact tone made me feel ashamed, as if maybe I were less than I should be. Frank must have picked up on it too, for he quickly added, "he's three years older than you, Mike."

I glanced back up to the window. The man was still there, but the hat was no longer waving. "I want to go into the hospital, see who the man is in the window."

"Maybe it's a woman," said John.

"I don't think so," I said. "You guys want to come in with me?"

"Not today," said Frank. We're going to John's. Maybe you should come with us, make sure you don't have any problem getting home."

I glanced over to the hospital window again and the man was gone. A strong wind slapped across my face and I thought about the warm register at home. I was curious about this mysterious person in the window but I also had a healthy fear of Rick Thornton. What if he was around when I came out alone?

"I am kind of cold," I said. "I guess I'll go with you guys."

SEVEN

Our kitchen was small. The cupboards were white but were badly in need of a fresh coat of paint. The stove and refrigerator were there before me and would most likely remain long after we had left, their feet sunken into the linoleum floor as if the appliances had put on weight over the years. There was limited counter space, but my mother kept it well organized. Her everyday items—meat grinder, colander, mixer—she kept out. The rest of her arsenal was either hung on the wall or stashed away. She was an excellent cook and got good use out of her kitchen. Our generation was not inundated with fast food, and people in general did not go out for meals as much as today and, even if they had, our lack of discretionary funds would have precluded our participation in any such ritual.

We had an A&W in town and a Dairy Queen, and we did frequent them on occasion, but that was it. During the summer we would make the occasional trip to my uncle's beer garden at the north end of town, but this was mostly to escape the heat on those evenings that just refused to cool down. They served cold sandwiches and coleslaw, sodas and a whole lot of beer. I have no other memories of going into a restaurant for dinner in my eleven years in Illinois.

The rear door to the house opened onto the small landing above the cellar stairs, adjacent to the kitchen. A chain had been draped across the stairwell as a safety measure, for if one were to be standing on the landing when the door opened there would be nowhere to go but down. A handrail had also been installed as a backup safety measure. None of this of course was foresight. When my parents first bought the house—before I was born—my Uncle Charlie was coming up the stairs from the cellar and had just reached the landing when my father opened the back door into his face. Fortunately, my uncle's jacket somehow got caught on the doorknob and stopped him from taking a nasty fall.

Another door, in the south wall of the kitchen, led to the only bathroom in the house, a very small room with barely enough space to turn around. The sink, toilet, and tub were old, the porcelain worn through in spots. The only window was cut high in the wall above the tub and was kept closed during the winter. It was perpetually fogged up and allowed for only a tiny, dream-like view of treetops and telephone wires. A long string had been hung from the ceiling so that anyone leaving an unpleasant odor behind could strike a match and burn a short section of the string. Ironically, the smell of the burning string carried much further throughout the house than any other noxious fumes, often exposing the perpetrator and making him/her the brunt of a cutting remark: "Carol just died in the bathroom," or "Dad's not constipated anymore." Fortunately, we all had the good sense to avoid this unpleasantness while meals were being prepared or consumed (well, most of the time).

———

My mother was preparing dinner when I came in. She would often times do her cooking in the early afternoon, especially if she was making a sauce; she liked to let it simmer for hours. She was of German heritage but my father's family had passed along numerous Italian recipes to her, most of which she had improved upon. She was an excellent cook and even though she had been off work from the hospital for a while to have the baby, she would still prepare large batches of soup or stew once a week and send them over with my father. She had passed her recipes along to Rose, but for some reason the final dish was never quite the same and the staff and patients alike had become spoiled. The hospital paid for the food and paid my mother for her time, even though she had offered her services for free.

"What are you making?" I asked.

"Spaghetti sauce."

She scooped a spoonful out of the pan and gently blew across it.

"Here, taste it," she said.

I took a small taste.

"Too salty?" she asked.

"No, it's good. Is that for us or the hospital?"

"This is for us," she said and returned to her work. When I picture my mother in that house, it is usually in the kitchen. She wears an apron adorned with pictures of farm animals—mostly chickens—her pink slippers and, depending on the time of day, either the terry-cloth robe or a rather plain dress with a soft open collar. She moves from cupboard to stove to refrigerator like a well-trained ballerina, each step a natural act of grace. Her tools are well worn: the heavy iron skillet, black as coal; wooden spoons, singed and misshapen from wear; an array of dulled and dented aluminum pots. She does not sing while she works but she does not begrudge the labor either. There is a deep-rooted acceptance, a feeling of belonging. It is as natural to her as the gentle sweep of her backhand to wipe away the sweat.

"Frank stopped a fight at Clark Street today."

"That boy and his fighting..."

"He wasn't in the fight, mom. Ricky Thornton was beating up on another kid and Frank made him stop. You shoulda seen it. Frank grabbed him by the neck and pulled him off. I thought for sure Thornton was gonna hit him, but he just walked away. It was great."

"There's nothing great about fighting. You better get out of those wet clothes. Where's your brother?"

It was no use. Mothers just don't appreciate a good fight.

"He's over at John's house. He should be home pretty soon. Who's the man in the yellow hat?" I asked. She grabbed an onion from the drawer and began dicing it.

"The only men in yellow hats I know are the ones who work with your father."

Martin coughed and the sound echoed from the dining room. I turned and looked in that direction and then back toward my mother, who stopped her work, wiped her eyes with a towel—from the onion, I suspect—and continued on with her work.

"The man at the hospital," I said.

"I don't know," she said. "Maybe it's a new patient."

"He's on the ground floor," I said. "Where they keep the ones who are dying."

She stopped her work abruptly and turned toward me.

"Who told you that?"

"I heard you talking to dad."

My father had said you could always tell how sick a patient was by which floor they kept them on. The morgue was in the basement, so naturally they kept the terminal cases on the first floor. Frank said they should keep the sickest ones on the top floor so they'd be closer to God. "What about the ones who aren't going to heaven?" I asked. "Put them on the roof," said Frank. "Let the devil work a little harder."

Martin coughed again, but deeper this time and congested. My mother wiped her hands on a dishtowel and moved toward the dining room. I followed her. She lifted Martin from his bassinet and held him close to her chest as she gently patted his back. His breathing was gurgled and sporadic. A tear-size droplet of mucus trickled from one nostril. His tiny eyes peered over her shoulder at me. They looked pitch-black.

"I don't know any man with a yellow hat," she said quietly, somewhat irritated. "Now go change your clothes."

Martin closed his eyes and pressed his head against my mother's shoulder. The porch door slammed shut and Martin raised his head again as Frank barged into the dining room, his wet boots tracking snow behind him.

"What's cooking?" he asked.

My mother looked down at the wet floor, as did Frank, and then their eyes met.

"I'm going, I'm going," he said and backed out of the room and onto the porch.

"And get a towel and wipe up this water, Frank..."

"Yeah, yeah..."

"How many times do you have to be told?"

"Once is more than enough," he said.

"You kids are driving me crazy."

"I didn't do anything," I said.

The kitchen door opened and Mrs. Grady's familiar voice rang out. "Yoo, hoo, Helen."

The screen door slammed shut behind Mrs. Grady, the noise echoing through the house like a gunshot. My mother took a deep breath and replied. "In the dining room."

70

I could hear metal banging in the kitchen and it occurred to me that it was taking Mrs. Grady a long time to make that short walk. She appeared at last, wrapped in a heavy winter coat with a wool scarf over her head and ears. There were melting snowflakes on her head—a welcome site to me—and a small bag in hand.

"I turned up the heat and took the lid off of your sauce," she said. "Better to let it breath."

Martin sneezed.

"That don't sound too good," said Mrs. Grady. "Is he okay?"

"The baby's fine, Margaret. What can I do for you?" I could tell my mother was not in the mood for her.

Mrs. Grady extended the hand holding the bag. "Brought you some things for the baby, some mentholatum and some cough syrup."

Frank returned to the dining room and set his boots by the register. He had yet to wipe up the water on the floor.

"Margaret, I've raised five children…" My mother's chiding was cut short by a quick burst of sizzling pops from the kitchen.

"My sauce. Michael, run and turn off the fire. Frank, clean up that mess. Next time you track snow into this house, I'm going to bat your ears."

"Oh, right Helen. You and what army?"

The sauce had already put out the fire by the time I got to the kitchen. I turned off the knob and decided—being as I was there already—to do my mother a favor and move the pan to another burner and wipe up the spilled sauce. It was a large pan with two ear-like handles along the rim. In one quick motion I grabbed both handles tightly and lifted the pan a couple of inches above the burner. I didn't really feel the heat until I was half way across the stove, but when that signal hit my brain, I let go. And I screamed.

"Yeowww!"

The heavy laden pan smacked down hard on the edge of the burner in a thunderous clash of metal, and then, being slightly tilted, began a quick decent towards the floor. By sheer reflex, I reached out for it, grabbed the handles again and fell with it, my arms fully extended, sauce erupting across the floor to the refrigerator, and pouring over one hand. When we hit the floor the pan was still upright. I released the handles and gave it a light shove. More sauce splashed out onto the floor as the pan finally came to a rest, half empty now, the remaining sauce lapping up against its sides like displaced water in a fat man's pool.

I looked up to see my mother, Mrs. Grady, and Frank staring down in disbelief; even Martin cranked his head to see what had happened. My mother handed Martin to Mrs. Grady and bent down to me. She was slightly panicked and I was slightly in shock, too stunned to cry.

"Oh my God! Are you all right? What happened?" She grabbed a towel and wiped the sauce from my hand.

"I'm sorry. I was trying to move the pan. "

My mother helped me up.

"Let me see your hands. Frank, get a bowl of water. Hurry."

That hand—my left—was burned pretty badly. The fingers of my right hand were much less severe, the sauce being much hotter than the handles.

Frank brought her the bowl of water and my mother set it on the counter and quickly stuck my hand in it. "How did you end up on the floor?" she asked.

"I was trying to save the sauce." The pain was unbearable.

"This really burns, mom."

"The cold water will help. I'll get some salve. You should have just let it fall."

"Smooth move, ex-lax," said Frank.

My mother turned to Mrs. Grady. I could see the words forming just inside her lips, but Mrs. Grady beat her to it.

"Get some gauze and salve," she said. "I'm not much of a cook but let's not forget, I was a nurse." She handed the baby to my mother, gently pulled my hand from the water and examined my wounds. "He'll be fine, Helen. I've seen plenty worse."

My mother's eyes filled with tears but she managed to hold them in. Her anger, however, was set free to run. "You've seen worse! Did I ask you to turn up the fire, Margaret? Did I ask you to bring me cough syrup?"

Frank reached over and placed a hand on my mother's shoulder. "Mom, it was an accident."

I chirped in. "It was my own fault."

At this point, she let out the tears—it was like a summer downpour—handed Martin off to Frank and stormed out of the kitchen.

Mrs. Grady stuck my hand back into the bowl of water. "We'll leave that in there for a little while. Feeling any better?"

"A little," I said.

She glanced down at the half empty pan of sauce. "I best be going. I'm sorry about your hand, Michael. Tell your mother not to wrap it too tight." She hobbled out the back door.

————

All in all, things worked out okay. My mother put some salve on both hands and wrapped my left one with gauze,

Frank had to clean up the mess, and I was somewhat of a hero. After all, I had saved our dinner at great risk to myself. When I climbed into bed that night, I felt rather proud of myself even though I knew it was all an accident.

EIGHT

The following morning, my mother went next-door and apologized to Mrs. Grady for losing her temper. Yes, she was a meddler and a busy body and if she hadn't turned up the fire under the sauce I wouldn't have gotten burned but her actions had been well intended. "Intentions," said my mother, "make all the difference." My father, who was less forgiving, had a different take on it. "The road to hell is paved with good intentions," he said. "She should mind her own business."

Later that day my parents checked Martin back into St. Mary's, just as a precaution—or so we were told; his weight was not what it should be and they feared pneumonia. My mother decided to go back to work so she could be close to him, and at the same time bring in some much needed money, and while I felt bad about Martin going into the hospital, I was happy that my mother would be there, working. I spent a lot of time on Clark Street during Christmas vacation and it comforted me knowing she was close by. And there were the free hot lunches to consider.

We got out of school early on Friday for vacation so Peter and I grabbed our sleds and went over to Clark Street. My left hand was still bandaged and somewhat painful to the touch, but I'd been cooped up in school all week and was dying to get out in the snow. And there was still the stranger with the hat. Would he still be there?

We spent what was left of the afternoon on the hill; Peter joined in on a free-for-all while I, concerned for my hand, kept to myself, descending the hill in a leisurely manner, avoiding any confrontation with the other boys or any rough terrain. A couple of jumps had been fashioned near the edge of the road allowing the boys to get a good four to five feet off the ground. I was tempted to give them a go but held back. As the day drew to an end we went in to check with my mother about a ride home. We set our sleds just inside the front door so nobody would take them.

"I thought she wasn't working anymore."

"She wants to be by Martin."

"Oh. Who's Martin?"

I looked at Peter in disbelief. "The baby!"

"Well, you never told me his name."

Laurie Anderson, Richard's sister, was working the desk. She was a year older than Carol and it was she who had put the two of them together. The prettiest girl in town, she could have had her pick of boyfriends but word was she had it bad for Peter's brother, Pat, whose only concern of late was religion. It didn't seem fair. Football players lined up with their lettermen's jackets and class rings; college professors finagled her into their classes, and they say that after giving her a physical examination, Dr. Morrison left his wife on the long shot of winning her affections. (This, I found out later, was another story started by Mrs. Grady.)

She had been over to our house on numerous occasions, mostly to help Carol with homework, and I would take these opportunities to try and get as close to her as possible, to brush up against her, smell her long blonde hair, feel the heat from her breath against my flesh. I was in love.

I still felt that way now—two years after having met her—

as she smiled at me from behind the counter, even though I had long ago come to realize the futility of my desire.

"Hi, Michael," she said. "Hi, Peter. How's Pat?"

"I don't know," said Peter. "All he ever does is go to church and read the bible."

"Tell him to call me, okay?"

"I guess," said Peter.

I placed my bandaged hand on the edge of her desk, hoping for an opportunity to relay the story of my heroics upon her.

"Is my mom off soon?" I asked.

She looked at the clock. "Anytime now. Why don't you boys have a seat and I'll page her."

The word boy stuck in my heart like a knife. How could fate be so cruel to have allowed me to be born too late for her? Couldn't she see that I was different? That although I was eight years younger than her, I was the only one capable of giving her the love she deserved? Was she blind? Maybe... of course, it was the devotion to God she so admired about Pat. I could do that for her. Pat only cared about God, but I would do both.

"I've been thinking about being an altar boy," I said. (There was that word again.) She smiled. I might just as well have said I had a life long ambition to collect trash. Peter looked at me and just shook his head.

"Well, that's nice," she said, and then she dropped the bomb. "But you've still got plenty of time to make up your mind before you grow up."

She dialed the phone. I began tapping my fingers on her desk and started toying with the bandage on my wound, but still could not manage to get her attention.

"Hi, Rose, can you tell Helen her son is here. Thanks," she said and hung up the phone.

"Do you know which room the man with the yellow hat is in?" I asked.

"No, I don't think I do," she said. "But I just started back yesterday, for the holidays. Do you know his name?"

"No, he's on this floor though. Can we go down there and look for him?"

"No, Michael, I'm sorry, but kids aren't allowed in that wing. What happened to your hand?"

At last. I opened my mouth to speak but before I could get a word out, the bell to the elevator behind us rang and the doors pulled back. (There were only two buildings in our town that had elevators: the hospital and the Murray Building. Sometimes on a Saturday we would spend the whole day riding the one in the Murray Building, a four story business office with a hardware store on the ground floor.)

Peter and I both turned to look as the old man wheeled his chair out of the elevator and into the lobby, his lean, muscular arms pumping energy to the steel contraption like two black pistons. The bell to the second elevator rang and those doors also flew back, with a vengeance, and out stomped Ethyl, the head nurse. The man smiled at us and tipped his yellow baseball cap, grinned at Ethyl and sped off down the hall.

"Cornelius! Cornelius Brown, come back here!" yelled Ethyl as she set her huge body in motion. Peter and I took off in close pursuit. "Cornelius!" she yelled again, but he was pulling away. We passed Ethyl at the first turn in the hall and could hear the old man yelling.

"Clear the road, emergency vehicle."

In the rooms along the corridor, patients (those with enough strength) sat up in their beds. A few hacked out a dry cheer as he passed by, slowing on occasion to tip his hat. In all my previous visits to the hospital I had never walked that corridor before today, had never been that close to death. I proceeded with caution past the drawn curtains and open doors, braving an occasional glance at an eerie sight of tubes and white, sickly flesh; a blend of feces and ammonia drifted through the air like an invisible storm. I felt embarrassed.

Two orderlies appeared from the other end of the hall and Cornelius spun his chair around and headed back toward us.

"Clear the road," he said as he approached us. We pushed up against the wall, eyes bulging as the aged gladiator roared by.

All that strength and vitality appeared trapped there in that corridor of decay. His exuberance had rubbed off briefly on the other patients, but they now began to fall back to their cots. A little piece of his energy seemed to fall back with them.

Ethyl jiggled around the corner and planted herself directly in his path and for the first time I saw the syringe. He slowed his chariot as he reached her.

"End of the line," she said, gasping for breath, and I could see his head drop from behind, as if the true weight of those words had landed on his shoulders. We arrived with the orderlies, who immediately grabbed hold of him from either side; but he had already given up the fight.

"Just hold his arm," said Ethyl. "Pull up his sleeve. Now, Mr. Brown, this isn't going to hurt."

He looked up at us, or more precisely, at me. His eyes were almost black and the whites the palest of yellows. He had short, curly, grey hair and dark brown skin, very smooth, taut and shiny, not at all like most older people I had seen.

"I don't need no damn shot. It ain't the pain..." But he winced as she stuck it in him. "Ouch! Woman, be careful."

"Just hush, now," she said.

"Tryin' to kill me."

"Don't hurt him," I said.

"Now, you see what you've done," said Ethyl.

"I didn't do nothin'. You're the one stuck me with that damn needle."

"You've scared these boys. You should be ashamed."

"These boys ain't afraid. I've see 'em."

It was him. The man in the window.

He looked me directly in the eye. "Been wondering when you'd show up."

"Let's go, Neely," said the orderly, who began pushing him away down the hall. "Time for your nap."

"Don't feel like a nap," said Cornelius. "I'll nap when I'm dead," he added, the words lazily drifting out of his mouth; the shot was already having an effect. He turned his head back in our direction and managed a slight wave with his hand.

"Come and see me," he said, and then they disappeared around a corner.

I turned to Ethyl. "Who is he?"

"His name is Cornelius Brown," she said.

"He sure is a crazy old nigger," said Peter.

"Peter!" said Ethyl.

"You shouldn't call him that," I said.

"Well, that's what he is," said Peter. It was not spoken out of malice, but rather something far worse—ignorance. Ignorance and indifference. He had heard it used so often, had become so accustomed to it, that it had become commonplace. A nigger was a lower form of life, lower than his father. Didn't everyone know that? No one had bothered to explain its significance to him, certainly not his father, whom I had heard use the word more than once.

"Is he going to die?" I said.

"Now, you never mind yourself about who's going to die," said Ethyl. As I gazed down the hall toward the few remaining patients who had yet to return to their rooms, the gravity of the situation began to set in. This was something I didn't understand and did not want to see. It does not occur to us at this age that we will one day be transformed into one of these other creatures, spent of all our youth and illusions, or that, conversely, once upon a time all these sick, dying people were young and vital. Some of the truth of the situation must have been seeping into my consciousness, for I was instinctively afraid and felt a great urgency to remove myself.

My mother came around the corner. "There you are. I've been looking all over for you."

"We had a little excitement," said Ethyl. "Didn't we boys?"

Ethyl's voice snapped me from my daydream and I turned my attention toward my mother. I was eager to share my discovery with her.

"Mom, I met him. I met Cornelius."

"That's nice, Michael," she said, and looked inquisitively to Ethyl.

"Cornelius Brown. Colored man, came in a couple weeks ago. Big C."

"He's the man with the hat. The yellow hat," I said.

My mother obviously had other things on her mind.

"We have to go now, Michael. Rose is giving us a ride home. She's waiting."

Peter whispered in my ear.

"Where's Martin?" I asked

My mother's eyes veered strategically toward Ethyl.

"Martin's going to stay with us for a little while longer," she said.

"Peter wants to see him," I said.

"Not today," said my mother. "Peter, you can see him when he's feeling better, okay?"

Peter shrugged. My mother pulled her hat over her ears and wrapped the worn scarf around her neck.

"Rose is waiting," she said, and the three of us departed.

All I could think about on the drive home was Cornelius. He had recognized me from his window amongst all the others. How was that possible? Had we met before? I doubted that. The only Negroes I knew were the family around the corner from us on Spring Street and the few kids at our school. And he had told me to come and see him. Of course, that would mean braving that hallway again, an unpleasant experience at best. Perhaps I could find a way to circumvent that gauntlet. If not, I would have to somehow find the courage to face it, for I was determined to find out more about this strange old man.

NINE

I had hoped to find a Christmas tree when we got home that afternoon but it was not forthcoming. It seemed with each passing year we got ours later in the season, and it went without saying that ours would not be huge or plush. But they were for the most part acceptable—once my mother broke out all the decorations. I had long ago given up hope for a wealth of presents but I still looked forward to the tree and the lights, the familiar bulbs, strands of tinsel, and the tarnished angel that always adorned the top.

My father shuffled in around seven o'clock. He was a quiet man, with a tendency to turn his shoulders in and slump forward when he walked, making his five foot seven inch frame appear even shorter. He wore a brown suede jacket, a plaid long sleeve shirt—always unbuttoned—over a t-shirt, gray cotton slacks and of course when he worked, a yellow hat with a black brim and a shield that read Yellow Cab.

At that point in time, I still liked my father. This was not due to any particular closeness between us—we spent very little time together—but rather from my observations of his personality. He was stern with us in general—we were not allowed to talk at the dinner table, for example—but around adults he had an easy-going air about him, was quick to laugh or tell a joke—generally corny ones—and was, for the most part, humble. He was at his best, or so it seemed to me, when he was around his family and speaking Italian. The phone would ring and he would answer, "Ciao, Joe, come stai," and a huge smile would blossom on his face. I would imagine him, in those moments, walking the streets with his brothers in a small village in Sicily, not a care in the world.

His big flaw, it seemed to me, was his temper, which could flare up at any moment. I saw it used toward my mother and mostly against Frank and in most of those situations, without provocation. As I grew older and his anger increased and his mental health declined, I would become more and more estranged from him, an estrangement that would last until I was well into my thirties and finally capable of seeing him as just a man, stripped of the burdens and expectations placed on a father.

Being a taxi driver, he knew most everyone in town, was well liked by most and treated everyone, even the Campbells, a black family who lived around the corner from us, the same—with respect. There had been a conversation between him and my mother one night about a loan Mr. Campbell tried to get to buy a house on the west end of town. He had been turned down and my father said it was on account of him being colored.

"Hell, the sons of bitches would have given him the loan if the house was on Spring Street. They just don't want any coloreds over there."

"There's never been any Negroes in that part of town, Sam," said my mother.

"He's a good man. Got nice kids." His voice had dropped off at that point, like he wasn't talking to my mother anymore, but himself. "They wanna keep everyone in their place."

"Hi, you guys," he said as he dropped the few tips he'd collected into the jar on the mantle and removed his jacket and hat, the wavy gray hair spilling out over his collar.

Mary and I echoed a soft hello but Frank did nothing to acknowledge his presence. Carol got up and grabbed his jacket and hat from the chair. Frank turned his head a bit, took a deep breath and shook his head with disgust.

"How was work?" asked Carol.

"Oh, about the same. Where's your mother?"

"In the kitchen," she said, as she hung up the old coat and set the hat on the closet shelf. My dad left the room as quietly as he'd come in and we returned our attention to the TV. We had only had one for about six months but already a pattern was beginning to develop—dinner, dishes (for the girls), homework (if we were so inclined; it was rarely enforced) and then TV. We only had the three networks to choose from but there was always something good to watch. Steve Allen had a show, Ed Sullivan (I particularly liked the music numbers.) and I remember Ernie Kovacs, whom I thought was the funniest of all. On Saturday mornings I would sometimes watch cartoons, unless of course there was any snow on the ground. (Odd, in a way, that I seemed to spend more time outdoors in the winter than I did in summer.)

If I got real lucky there would be a Lash Larue film. Lash was a cowboy who carried a whip and rode what I presumed to be a purple horse. I don't know if it was our particular television, or just the black and white film that cast that hue, but for me his horse was and always will be purple.

I got up during a commercial and went to the window to see if perhaps a tree was tied onto the car but it was too dark to tell.

"If you're looking for a tree," said Frank, "you might as well forget it."

"It's only two weeks till Christmas," I said.

"Well, the old cheapskate will probably wait till the day before so he can save a dollar."

"Watch your mouth," said Carol.

Frank mumbled a response but I couldn't make it out. Mary kept her eyes on the tube throughout. Carol was about to go after Frank; I could see it in her eyes. A fight between them would quickly bring my father back, a situation which I had no desire to see develop. Since the war between Frank and my dad had begun—when had it all started?—I had learned to foresee trouble and diffuse it whenever possible.

"Is Anna gonna be here this Christmas?" I asked.

"Mom said she'd be here a couple of days before," said Carol, who then turned and left the room. I took a deep breath and looked over toward Mary, who for the first time since my father's arrival took her eyes off the TV and glanced my way, eyebrows raised. Another close call.

———

Later that evening, Frank sat on the bed carving up a bar of Ivory soap. It looked like another horse head (his favorite subject). How he managed these carvings was a mystery to me, for he had nothing to guide him, no picture or statue to copy. He would take a bar of soap and just start into it, and a few hours later he would have a beautiful horse head or a dog or a pigeon. As I recall, all of his carvings were of animals.

I got my three-by-fives and my baseball cards from my drawer, determined to start my World Series. But first, there were improvements to be made in the game. Throughout the season, it had been a hitter's league. Batting averages ran as high as four hundred. Gil Hodges had hit thirty homeruns in fifty games, and the best E.R.A. in the league was posted by Whitey Ford, who somehow managed a meager 3.5.

The first thing I had to do was add more strikes; in a stack of one hundred twenty cards there had only been thirty. I added ten more. I also removed two of the home-run cards, added two singles, one ground out, a double play, and created an additional sub-pile for long fly balls. Whenever the long fly ball card turned up in the main pile, I would shuffle the sub-pile, which consisted of half a dozen cards, and draw the top one. The options were: home-run; ball is caught—all runners hold; ball is caught—runners advance; ball is caught—tagging is optional, see tag pile; ball hits the wall for a double—all runners advance two bases; great catch—flip a coin to see if base runners are doubled up. There were other sub-piles for stolen bases, bunting, and wild pitch. These had been utilized throughout the season and seemed to function quite well.

The only other addition was an injury card, which had to show up twice during a game in order for it to be activated. On the second drawing, a card would be drawn from a sub-pile determining the nature and severity of the injury.

After making the changes, I ran a few practice games to see if any additional alterations were necessary. In five games, I had one shutout, one minor injury, an extra inning game and only seven home runs. I was ready.

The series would open in New York. I put Drysdale on the mound against Whitey Ford. Drysdale had had a bad year in '58, but what Dodger pitcher hadn't? He'd done well in '57, and was, as far as I was concerned, the best L.A. had to offer. (Koufax would not really come on strong until '59.) The line-up went as such: Gilliam led off at third; Neal at second; Hodges at first; Snider batting cleanup, playing center; Furillo in right; Cimoli in left; Campanella, Reese, and Drysdale.

I can't really say when my infatuation with the Dodgers began. We lived a thousand miles from New York, and I had certainly never been to one of their games. We were only a hundred miles from Chicago and I had never made it up there to see a ball game either. In fact, the idea that I might actually some day attend a major league baseball game never crossed my mind. That possibility was as foreign to me as the rest of the world outside the borders of our small town.

Still, somehow, I had picked the Dodgers as my team. Perhaps I had seen a game on TV and something about the team or some player caught my eye. Like I said, I don't recall there being any definitive moment, but they were, for me, the only team to follow, and my favorite player on that team was Gil Hodges, the first basemen, whom Vince Scully referred to as The Quiet Man. He had large hands and thus was perfectly suited for his position at first base, winning more than one golden glove award. He was also good with the bat, always hitting in the high 200's with 350 lifetime homeruns. Despite his achievements with the glove and the bat he never made it to the Hall of Fame, a slight that still irritates me to this day. But, more importantly to me than all his baseball prowess was his disposition. I listened to almost every game on my transistor radio, and watched as many as opportunity would allow on TV. Never did I see him yell at an umpire or hear Scully mention any such encounter. He was a gentlemen and a good ballplayer, and to me a hero.

For the Yankees, I followed their actual '58 World Series roster. And what a roster! Mantle, Berra, Bauer, McDougald. It had the makings of a great series.

I set the Yankee cards in the field and shuffled the stack of three-by-fives. (I had numerous Mickey Mantle cards but I chose his rookie card to place in the field; I wasn't a Yankee fan but Mickey was special.) Something light hit me in the head and I looked down to see a piece of Ivory soap on the floor. I looked up at Frank.

"I'm turning out the light," he said.

"But I gotta play this game."

"You've been playing it for two hours. I wanna go to sleep."

"I'll be quiet."

"I can't sleep with the light on."

I gave in. I was feeling kind of tired, myself. I left the players in the field and crawled into bed. There were chips of soap everywhere.

"There's soap in the bed, Frank."

"What's wrong with that, it'll keep you clean." he said and turned out the light.

I lay there quietly for a few minutes, thinking about my World Series, about Cornelius Brown and about my dad.

"Are you still awake?"

"Yeah, why?"

"Can I ask you a question?"

"What?"

"Why are you and Dad always fighting?"

"He doesn't like me and I don't like him."

"Why?"

"Because he's an asshole."

"But, why doesn't he like you?"

"He doesn't like me because I don't feel sorry for him and I won't kiss up to him."

"But sometimes you're the one that starts the fight."

"That doesn't make him any less of an asshole. Try not to worry about it too much. In a few more years I'll be gone."

"Where?"

"Anywhere. Now go to sleep."

"Do you think I kiss up to him?"

Frank sighed. "I don't know. No, I don't. You're a good kid. Don't worry about it. Now, I'm going to sleep."

I tried my best to fall asleep, but I couldn't help wondering just what exactly it was between them and what he meant by not feeling sorry for my dad. And I needed to pee. I looked over at Frank. He had already begun to doze off and I was afraid if I got up I might disturb him. I tried counting backwards from one thousand, figuring if I could just fall asleep, maybe I could wait until morning. But the pain grew worse and at nine hundred and eighty I crawled out of bed.

"Where you going?" asked Frank, half asleep.

"To the bathroom."

There was a light on downstairs and as I reached the bottom I could hear my parents' voices in the dining room. I sat on the bottom step, listening.

"Maybe it won't last that long," said my mother.

"Reynolds says there's probably going to be more layoffs at Owens next week. They lost a huge contract."

"It's Christmas. People always use taxis this time of year."

My fathers voice grew louder. "I had half my regular fares today, Helen. And this is only the first day of the layoff."

"What if we open the nursery? I could take in a few kids on the weekend."

"You don't understand. Everybody's cutting back. Nobody's going to bring their kids here. It's a luxury."

It was quiet for a minute and then my father started up again. "How's the baby doing?"

"Dr. Levin says he doesn't have pneumonia...yet. He wants to keep him in the hospital, just to be sure."

"I don't know how the hell we're going to pay for all this."

"Maybe you need to talk to Charlie about a loan."

"No. Absolutely not."

My mother began to cry. "He's your brother..."

"I won't give him the satisfaction."

As quickly as the crying started, it stopped again, as she tried to exert her will on him. "These kids have got to have a Christmas."

I got up from my seat and started up the stairs.

"They'll survive."

It was my mother's turn to raise her voice. "That's not enough, Sam," she said as I made the turn at the top of the stairs and moved beyond the range of their voices.

I climbed back into bed. Frank turned over and complained. "Mind if I get some sleep, now."

"Sorry," I said.

"Sweet dreams," said Frank.

I lay awake for quite some time, running my parents' conversation through my head, fearful now that there might not be any Christmas at all for us, least of all, a new glove for me. Once I was sure Frank was asleep, I quietly slid out of bed, opened the bottom dresser drawer and retrieved a flashlight. I needed to put my thoughts elsewhere.

The Dodgers drew first blood. Gilliam opened up the first inning with a single. Neal bunted him to second and after Hodges flew out, Snider hit one over the center field fence. Furillo and Cimoli made outs. I started shuffling the cards for the bottom of the inning. Questions flooded my mind. How could it be that people needed a ride one day and then suddenly could do without it the next? What if the Owens plant were to close down, altogether? Would my dad be out of work, like Peter's? Would the man still drive his truck down our driveway and deliver the coal to the bin in our cellar? Would we have to move to California?

The Dodgers held their 2-0 lead until the bottom of the seventh. With the bases loaded and two out, a pinch hitter was brought in to bat for Ford, who had pitched brilliantly since the first inning, allowing only three hits and striking out eight. But he had to go; no pitcher would be allowed to bat under those circumstances.

Of course, a pinch hitter meant a shuffled deck. There were only three reasons to shuffle: one was, of course, after each half inning; the others were for a change in pitchers or for a pinch-hitter. Bobby Richardson, of all people, came up to the plate and hit the first pitch—long fly ball. I grabbed the sub-pile, shuffled it, closed my eyes and turned over the top card, calculating the odds (only one chance in six of a home run). Please, God! But it was futile. I may as well have been praying to my transistor radio. The Yankees were leading 4-2, and they held that lead to win it. Game one had not gone well.

I left the cards on the floor and climbed into bed. A few minutes later my parents tiptoed through our room on their way to their bedroom. I recalled the pain in my bladder and rushed downstairs to use the toilet. The odor hit me half way down the stairs. It was my father's, easily recognizable—he was the only one in the house who drank beer—and exceptionally pungent this evening. Why hadn't he lit the string? I backed up the steps, took a deep breath and raced to the bathroom where I held my nose with one hand and my penis with the other. There in the dark, with the pain streaming out, I ran out of air before piss and my father's bitter aroma rushed in.

TEN

I walked to work with my mother the following morning, dragging my sled along behind me. The air was cold
and sharp and snapped at my ears and nose. The late night
showed on my mother's face, but despite her lack of sleep
she seemed in a good enough mood. The two of us had
eaten a quick breakfast of oatmeal and toast and then quietly
slipped out the side door, leaving the rest of the family fast
asleep when we left.

"Why don't you take the car?"

"Your father might need it later. Besides, I don't like driving when it's icy."

I wanted to ask her about the conversation she and my
father had, if maybe they had figured out a way to buy presents, but I couldn't figure out a way to bring it up, and if I
did I'd have to explain how I happened to be eavesdropping
from the stairs, an invasion of privacy highly frowned upon
by my mother. I decided to let it be and focus on the day
before me.

I would walk for a ways then hop on my sled whenever
the road looked clear and go for a short ride, then turn
around and sled back to her. Or a beam of light would break
through the veil of clouds and I would hurry to the spot and
stand facing the sky to warm my face, my mother maintaining her cautious pace over the icy walk throughout my

excursions, leaving me free to wonder about haphazardly like a rubber ball tied to a paddle by an invisible string.

The town was very quiet at this time of morning without the racket of school children hustling along to class. I could hear the scratch of squirrels' feet digging into the bark of the trees as they scurried along, seemingly without order or purpose, their jerky movements like actors in a silent film. I watched in awe as one leaped through space, floating weightlessly from one tree to another.

As we reached St. Anthony's, I purposely sledded ahead of my mother, taking the long route so as to direct her away from the grounds (I hadn't gone to church as promised.), although today she seemed engrossed in thought and would probably have missed the shortcut anyway. Having dodged the church I sped ahead for a while on my sled until finally joining up with her at the hospital entrance.

"Are you coming in?" she said.

"In a while." There were a few kids at the top of the hill and I wanted to get in some runs. "How late are you working?"

"Just till noon, today. We can walk home together."

"Okay," I said. "See you later."

"Be careful of your hand."

I looked down at my wrapped left hand. It didn't hurt anymore but it was still wrapped with gauze. My mother had made a point of cleaning it everyday since the accident and every time she did so she would look up at the sky and shake her head in disgust, a gesture no doubt meant for Mrs. Grady.

She went inside and I stood for a moment watching her until she vanished from my sight, then I headed toward the top of the hill. There were only a handful of boys, not enough for teams, so everyone mostly just kept to themselves. Someone had fashioned a couple of banks to one side of the road, which allowed for some exciting jumps, but all in all it was somewhat boring. My parents' conversation kept playing in my head like a bad song. I wanted to be free of it, wanted to put my thoughts elsewhere.

I was standing at the top of the hill by myself, contemplating one more run, when it hit me, smack in the middle of my left ear. The impact almost knocked me off my feet. This was not your standard snowball that dissolves upon impact, leaving a light sting and white marker behind, but a heap of snow that had been kneaded and compacted into a dense ball of ice. (I had seen a boy lose an eye once by just such a ball.) It felt like my head had been slammed against the pavement, the pain extending inside my ear to the middle of my head. I screamed and tears filled my eyes as I lifted my hand to my ear and started toward the hospital. I could hear laughter coming from my left but I paid little attention to it as I was consumed by pain and a desire for relief.

Laurie was working the desk and when I entered the hospital and saw her I tried to suck up the tears; but it was too late. She came around from her desk and put her soft white hand on my head.

"What happened?"

I still held my gloved hand to my ear. "I got hit by an iceball," I said, and she pulled my hand away from my ear.

"Let me see." She placed her warm hand on the side of my face and for a moment the pain went away.

"Sit down over here," she said. "Let's see if we can clean this out."

I sat behind her desk, her silky hair caressing my cheek, as she picked the remaining ice from my ear with a cotton swab.

"Feeling a little better?"

"It still stings a little," I said, trying to downplay the intense pain.

"You should have a doctor look at it."

"That's okay," I said. "It'll be alright. Thanks."

"Okay, if you're sure. Why don't you have a rest before you go back out, though."

"Okay," I said and walked over to sit down. After about two minutes of thumbing through some grown-up magazines I got bored and decided to visit the old man, Cornelius. I hadn't seen him in the window that morning.

I waited for Laurie to leave her post and then quickly made my way across the lobby and down the hall, eyes straight ahead at all times so as not to gaze upon any of the sickly residents inhabiting that wing. My ear was still throbbing and sounds crackled from the water trapped within as I reached his room, the door slightly ajar.

I tapped lightly but there was no answer so I pushed it open and stepped inside. There was an empty bed directly inside the door, and a second bed closer to the window, the curtain between them partially drawn so that only half of the second bed was exposed to my view. I stepped quietly toward the bed till at last I could see him, fast asleep, one arm connected to a bottle of liquid by a long rubber tube. On the table beside the bed lay the yellow hat. I stood for a moment watching him. Outside, in the distance, boys began their descent down Clark Street, and then quickly disappeared behind the trees.

I turned to leave the room. "Where you going?" he said and I jumped, somewhat startled by his voice, and turned around.

"Nowhere. I didn't want to wake you up."

"Well, I'm already awake. Come over here, boy."

I inched my way to the foot of the bed, my eyes darting back and forth from Cornelius to the hat. He looked smaller, there in the bed, than he had that day in the wheelchair.

"What's so damn interesting?"

"I don't know."

"You never see a black man before?"

"Oh, yes, sir. There's lots of colored folks live here."

"Coloreds, huh?"

I was drawn to the hat like a magnet. It was not nearly as bright up close as it appeared in the window. It was turned so I couldn't quite make out the letters.

"You like the hat?"

"Just wondered what it says."

He reached over with his free arm and grabbed it. "Says Giants. That was my team."

"New York Giants?"

"No. Chicago."

"Chicago? I never heard of any Chicago Giants."

"No, I don't suppose you have. That was a long time ago. Negro League."

I had never heard of such a thing. I knew there was an American League and a National League and of course the minors, but no one had ever mentioned anything to me about any Negro League. I pretended to understand.

"Oh," I said.

"I guess you never heard of that before, either, huh, boy?"

"Well, sir, not very much. Is that in a different Chicago than the Cubs?

He smiled. "In a manner of speaking. Maybe someday I'll tell you about it. What's your name boy?"

"Michael Carmello."

"Carmello? What's that—Italian?"

"Yes, sir."

"I'm Cornelius Brown. Friends call me Neely."

He stuck out his hand to shake. It was huge but his grip was weak.

"You a ballplayer?"

"I'm gonna try out for Little League this year. If we don't move to California, that is."

"What's wrong with California. They got Little League there, don't they?"

For some reason, I had never thought of it before. I knew they had an ocean and of course the Dodgers had just moved there, but other than that, I rather thought that life as I knew it would not exist in a place where the sun was out year round.

"I guess so," I said. "I just don't want to move."

"Well, I've been there. I've seen worse. How old are you, boy?"

"Eleven."

"Eleven?" He looked me up and down. I expected him to mention my size; I'd heard it all before—more than once.

"How come you waited so long to play?"

"I don't know. I'm not very good."

"You're not, huh? What position you like to play?"

"Pitcher."

He looked down at the bandages. "What happened to your hands?"

I told him about the accident. "Was it worth it?"

"What?"

"The spaghetti dinner. Was it worth the pain?"

"My mother makes the best sauce."

He laughed. "Well, there you go."

He grabbed my right arm. "You right handed?"

"Yes, sir."

"Don't gotta call me sir, son. Name's Neely. Pitcher's got to have a strong arm of course, and good legs. Don't particularly have to be big. Lot of guys I knew weren't that big, could still throw the ball ninety miles an hour." He reached down to his blanket and pulled it up to his chin. "Gettin' a little chilly in here, don't you think?"

He seemed, in that instant, to grow weaker, his body retreating deeper into the bed. I looked up at the bottle connected to his arm.

"Are you real sick?"

"That's what they tell me. I just mostly get tired. You ever do around-the-world with a yo-yo and after a couple of times around it kinda slows down?"

I nodded.

"Well, I'm just like that yo-yo. I wanna keep goin' 'round and 'round but I can't. Guess I need a new string."

He grabbed hold of the tube leading to his arm.

"Maybe I could use this," he said, and started to laugh but the laugh turned into a violent cough and I backed away from the bed. His eyes filled with tears. He grabbed a handful of tissue from the table and held them to his mouth and slowly his coughing subsided.

"It's okay," he said, his voice rough and cracking. He reached over and grabbed the hat. "You wanna try it on?"

I hesitated.

"Go ahead. Won't bite you."

I slipped the old hat on and it fell down over my ears, bringing a smile to Cornelius's face. I handed it back to him.

"It's too big," I said.

He inspected the hat closely, very seriously, as if he were looking for flaws in it.

"No," he said. "I think your head's too small."

I laughed again, but stopped quickly for fear he might start coughing again.

"Hey. Your old man showing' you how to throw the ball?"

Like any eleven year old boy, I would have loved answering yes, to tell of the hours spent together in the backyard, practicing. But the truth was, my father didn't take much of an interest other than to mention the one-in-a-million chance of anyone making it to the majors. It wasn't even personal enough wherein he had evaluated my ability and then sat me down and said look, this is how it is, kid, you just don't have it. It was more like, those things only happen to other people, so why waste your time trying. Get a job, make a living.

"No," I said, trying to cover, "my dad's pretty busy most of the time."

He stared at me for a few seconds. I couldn't meet his eyes.

"Well, hell, I know what that's like. A man can't do everything he wants to do. You don't suppose he'd mind if I was to show you a few things, do you?"

I couldn't believe my ears. I had never met a professional ball player before—had never even been to a Major League game—had actually never even seen one in person, and now here was one ready to take his time to teach me. I didn't hesitate.

"Could you really? That would be great."

My excitement passed quickly as the reality of the situation exploded in my head. There was no way Cornelius was going outside to play baseball.

"Where would we do it?" I asked.

"That's for me to worry about," he said. "You got a ball and a glove?"

"Sure."

"You bring 'em with you next time you come."

The noon bells started ringing at St. Anthony's and Cornelius turned to look out the window. You couldn't see the church from his room, so the bells seemed to just emanate from the heavens. At some point in our conversation it had begun to snow but I had only just now noticed it.

"You better be runnin' along now, boy. My string's starting to wind down again."

"Okay, I'll see you tomorrow."

I stopped as I reached his door and turned around. His eyes were closed and his chin rested on his chest. In the distance, the bells finished their countdown to noon. I took off looking for my mother, the pain in my ear long forgotten.

ELEVEN

I was up early the next morning hoping to get out of the house before my mother could get a chance to slow me down. No such luck. I waited impatiently while she fixed me some scrambled eggs, which I then downed as quickly as possible, loaded my glove and ball into a small pack and took off. I ran into Peter and Jimmy Ryerson at the corner, on their way downtown. I liked Jimmy. He lived across town in a nice house and his dad made a lot of money, but he was always nice to me, as were his parents. He was bigger than either Peter or myself—of course, we were both on the small side—and he was a good ballplayer.

"We're going to the toy store. Wanna go?"

"I'm going to see Neely. Besides, the store's not open yet."

"We're gonna ride the elevator in the Murray Building till it opens," said Jimmy. "Who's Neely?"

"He's a professional baseball player. His name is Cornelius Brown but his friends all call him Neely. He's gonna show me some pitches."

"He's a nig...he's colored," said Peter.

"What team's he on?"

"From the Negro Leagues," I said, as if it—the Negro League—was common knowledge. "And he isn't on any team now. He's old."

"Oh," said Jimmy. "That sounds pretty good. Not the old part, I mean."

"You can come if you want," I said, hoping he would decline. Right now I was sorry I brought it up. I didn't really feel like sharing my new friend.

"Nah, it's okay. We're going into town. Maybe some other time."

"Why don't you forget that old guy and come with us," said Peter.

"No thanks," I said. "See you guys later." I quickly departed before either of them could change their mind.

———

Ethyl wouldn't let me in to see Cornelius. She said he'd been up most of the night and had just gotten to sleep.

"Can I see him when he wakes up?"

"It may be a while, Michael. Maybe tomorrow would be better."

"Oh. What's the big C?"

"What?"

"You told my mom he had the big C. What's that?"

Ethyl took a deep sigh and put a hand on my shoulder. "I guess you're old enough to know. It's cancer. Mister Brown has cancer in his lungs."

"Is he gonna die?"

"Everybody dies, Michael. Only the good Lord knows when. As for Mister Brown, my guess is he doesn't have much time left on this Earth. Now you run along like I said and come back tomorrow."

I didn't leave immediately but rather hung around the lobby, nervously tossing the baseball into the well formed pocket of my old mitt. After a while I started throwing it up in the air, higher and higher with each toss, catching it backhand, then behind the back, feeling quite pleased with myself, until finally I missed, the ball caroming off my glove and rolling over to the desk where the girl, who had watched my performance in angst, took a deep breath, tapped her pencil a few times against the tabletop and reached down to retrieve the ball.

"You shouldn't play ball indoors," she said. I had never seen her before.

"Where's Laurie?"

"I don't know. She's not working today. Are you waiting to see someone?"

"Yeah. Sort of. Can I have my ball?"

"Well, if you're going to wait, please don't throw the ball. You might break something." She handed it to me.

"Thanks." I returned to my seat but after a few torturous minutes of inactivity decided to leave and join Peter and Jimmy, downtown.

I noticed the smoke shortly after leaving the hospital; the huge charcoal colored cloud stood out against the light gray sky, its funnel touching down over the city like a tornado. Traffic had chewed up the snow on most of the streets, making sledding difficult and forcing me to occasionally dismount and drag my sled along behind me as I hurried toward the fire. In the distance I could hear the sirens and as I drew nearer I could see the police cars and the fire trucks; an ambulance raced by me and splashed my jeans with slush.

I arrived to see the Murray Building aglow, gigantic flames leaping from the windows, the glass exploding into bits and raining down upon the sidewalk. A large crowd had already gathered, the police working frantically to keep them away.

"Mister, what time is it?" I asked.

The man looked down at me, puzzled. "Jesus, kid, I don't know."

A woman stuck her head out of a fourth floor window and began screaming, her pleas for help cutting into my ears like ice. People pointed up at her. I recalled the opening to Superman. 'Look, up in the air. It's a bird, it's a plane...'

"There's a woman up there!"

"Oh, my God, she's trapped!"

She disappeared into the room and then seconds later eased one leg tentatively out the window, then another, and ever so slowly slid down the face of the brick wall to her armpits.

She looked straight down and then out toward the crowd.

"She's gonna jump!"

I turned and caught sight of the fire engine as it rounded the corner and pushed its way up the street. I wondered how I had managed to beat it there. When I looked back, the woman had lowered herself further and was now hanging from the windowsill by both hands, the strength gone from her screams, flames snapping at her fingers. The fire truck eased its way through the noisy crowd and came to a halt in front of the building. One man grabbed a hose and began pulling it from the truck toward the hydrant while three others raced toward the building. They were carrying some sort of contraption that they opened up into a circle as they approached the building. It was the size of a small trampoline. A couple of men from the crowd ran to their side to help.

Someone hollered, "Hold on!" There came another scream, the loudest yet, and then a series of "oohs" and "ahs" swept through the crowd as the woman, unable to maintain her grip, released and began her journey down the face of the building, grasping desperately at the protruding bricks, but unable to find a hold. Her dress blew up around her neck and head as she sped toward the ground like a broken umbrella, till at last she bounced off a window ledge, ripped through the awning above the entrance and slammed down onto the trampoline, the five men bent at the knees to absorb the shock. Her weight threw them all to the cold cement, but one by one they picked themselves up and somebody yelled "She's okay!" and the crowd cheered.

Others, I would find out later, were not so lucky.

I ran off to the toy store in search of Peter and Jimmy. As I had suspected, it was not yet open, and I began to fear the worst. But as I passed Hill's Drug Store I saw Jimmy sitting on the floor in front of the magazine rack, the latest Superman comic in hand. I looked around the store but could see no one else. They had evidently left the store unattended to go watch the fire.

"Where's Peter?"

"I don't know. Probably over at the Murray."

"I thought you were with him."

"We got in a fight, so I left."

"The Murray Building is burning down, Jimmy. Didn't you hear the sirens?"

Jimmy jumped to his feet. "You're kidding! Let's go."

He headed toward the door, comic in hand. "What about the book?" I said. He looked around the room, saw it was empty and stuffed the book into his pants.

"Do you think Peter got out?" Jimmy asked as we ran down the street.

"I hope so. I can't believe you didn't hear the sirens."

"I was reading. I didn't notice them."

By the time we got there, the crowd had been pushed back

a whole block from the fire, which continued to rage out of control. We wandered through the crowd looking for Peter, but he was nowhere to be found. We asked an ambulance driver if there had been a boy our age but he said it was too soon to tell, the fire was still too hot for them to go inside. We waited around another hour but they told us it would be morning before they searched for bodies. We headed for home, unable to truly grasp the tragedy before us, unwilling to accept Peter's death.

"What was the fight about?" I asked.

"I don't know," said Jimmy, a bit squeamishly.

"What do you mean, you don't know."

"He never has any money, and he always expects me to give him some. I offered to share my coke with him but he said he wanted his own. I told him no, so he punched me, and I left."

The thought that Peter's poverty may have taken his life and saved Jimmy's was unnerving. Fate was so fickle. What if I'd never met Cornelius? Would I have gone to the Murray building with them? Would I have shared with Peter? Would the three of us boys have perished together? I reached into my pocket. There were two dimes and a nickel. Enough to kill you?

Jimmy must have been reading my mind. "Just think," he said. "If I had bought Peter a coke, I might have been caught in that fire with him."

"Maybe he's okay," I said. "Maybe he got out."

"Maybe. I hope so. I like Peter, but you know how he is."

"Yeah, I know," I said. We continued on in silence for a few minutes, dragging our sleds behind us as we made our way away from town toward our homes. Every once in a while I would stop and look behind me thinking, I suppose, that he might be there. But all I saw was the empty sidewalk and a distant plume of dark smoke. I had lived four doors away from Peter my whole life. We argued a lot and got in a lot of fistfights, but he was still my best friend. The thought that I might never see him again was just too overwhelming to comprehend.

I said goodbye to Jimmy as he turned down Monroe Street toward his house, and continued on alone. I thought about Neely, lying in his hospital bed. What was it Ethyl had said? "Not much time left on this Earth." None of it made any sense. Everything was so random. At St. Anthony's we were told we had guardian angels looking after us. Where was Peter's?

The thought occurred to me that I should go back to the hospital and see Neely before something awful happened to him but I also felt completely exhausted. As I reached the end of our street I stopped and stared at Peter's house. I don't know what exactly I expected to see, some sign perhaps of Peter's demise, his mother sitting on the porch consumed by grief; or his father, how would he react? Would he break into a rage? Would he blame Peter for his own death? But there was nothing unusual. I neither saw nor heard any signs of any life coming from the house. I considered going up to the door and knocking, but if Peter wasn't there I would have to explain everything. That, I could not do.

I continued on to my house and went directly upstairs to my bed and fell asleep. When I awoke later that afternoon, I tried to get up the courage to call Peter's parents and tell them what had happened.

And then the phone rang. My mother called out to me.
"Michael, Peter's on the phone."
Peter never called me on the phone so my first reaction

was to doubt my mother.

"Are you sure it's Peter?"

"I think I know Peter's voice," she said. She was busy putting dishes away in her curio.

"What's the matter? You look shocked." I had not said a word to anyone about the day's activities, although by now my mother had surely heard about the fire.

"Nothing's wrong, " I said. I picked up the phone and spoke quietly into the mouthpiece.

"Hello?" My mother stopped what she was doing and watched me with unusual interest.

"Peter! I thought you were dead."

At the word dead, my mother dropped a plate to the floor. But by some good fortune, it caught the edge of the rug and bounced onto the wood, undamaged. My mother glanced down to the plate and then back at me. She must have seen something in my face that told her to leave me be, for she just reached down and picked up the plate and left the room.

"You won't believe what happened," he said.

Shortly after Jimmy had left for the drug store, Old Man Meyers had come out of his office and told Peter he had to quit riding the elevator. Meyers was sort of a combination custodian/guard for the building. A retired policeman, he seemed to get as much pleasure chasing us out of the building as we got from harassing him.

Rather than leave the building, Peter had decided to take one last ride to the top floor where he then got out of the elevator and proceeded by way of the staircase to the roof. There were always hundreds of pigeons up there—in fact, the sidewalk around the building was splattered with droppings—and in the winter it was easy to catch them as they huddled together in the corners for warmth. After chasing pigeons around for a while (without any success) he had pulled a piece of cardboard up against a wall to take a rest and ended up falling asleep.

He awoke shortly thereafter enveloped in black smoke, fumes from the melting tar searing his eyes and lungs, and began probing his way through the thick cloud towards what he hoped was the rear of the building, tripping once over an air vent and smashing down hard on his hands and knees. From behind him came a tremendous rumble as the whole mid-section of the roof collapsed. He looked back to see the flames spewing forth from the hole. Another section went. It was as though he were on top of a volcano.

He reached out and grabbed what he hoped was the steel ladder at the top of the fire escape. Yes! There was hope. Quickly, clumsily, he made his way down the ladder, missing the final step and falling to the landing at the fourth floor. A window exploded and flames leaped out as if it were even too hot inside for them. On his feet again, he continued his blind descent, not knowing if the fire escape was completely intact, if the next step might be his last. As he got closer to the bottom, visibility improved. He reached the second floor only to discover there was no longer a ladder leading to the ground, at which point he had to hang from the landing and drop the final ten feet, spraining an ankle in the process—his only injury; well, that and an ear-boxing he got from his old man when he found out what happened. It was a beating Peter took with a smile.

———

Four people died in the fire. There had been an odor of gas that morning when everyone arrived for work at the hardware store. Employees complained and asked to be let off work but were told if they left they couldn't come back. Nobody left. There was an explosion and then the fire, spreading quickly throughout the building. Old Man Meyers was found in the elevator, stuck on the third floor. He had not burned but rather melted from the intense heat. The lady who had jumped and been caught by the firemen suffered a broken hip and arm. Mr. Lewis, the manager who refused to let anyone leave, was out having coffee when the fire started.

TWELVE

My oldest sister, Anna, had entered the convent when she was nineteen, creating quite a controversy in our house, for my mother was adamantly opposed to it and had even gone so far as to question Anna's sanity.

My mother, who's only ambition in life was to have a large family, to watch her children grow, was losing her oldest daughter to the church, a church she had no part in, a religion for which she had no need. She had agreed to the "deal" as a matter of appurtenance. She never imagined it would come to this, that the religion would actually take hold of her children, affect their lives in any profound way. We were packed off to Catholic school, paraded through the sacraments, the Trinity, the beauty of Christ, the fear of God. Seven hours a day, five days a week we were indoctrinated with this belief system, only to arrive home each afternoon to indifference, as if we would drop it at the door as we entered the house, as we would our dirty boots.

I was eight at the time and I remember the morning Anna departed. It had been hot and extremely humid the day before and I had not slept well that night, but I still managed to drag myself out of bed at six o'clock to see her off. My mother refused to go with us to the depot, and would not even come out of her room to say good-bye.

My father carried her one small suitcase out to his cab

while Anna said her farewells to everyone. She kept looking toward the staircase, expecting, I suppose, my mother to have a last minute change of heart, but it was not to be.

I rode with them to the depot, a very slow, solemn drive with me in the back seat trying to think of something to say and Anna staring pensively out the window. My father told her a little about St. Louis—that's where she was headed—how he had been there a few times when he and his brothers still had their band, that it wasn't a bad city but she had to stay out of certain areas. Anna remained, for the most part, silent.

The train rumbled in from the north, a silver Santa Fe with a red and yellow face, the engine screamed past us to the end of the station so that for a second I thought perhaps it would continue on and Anna would not have to leave. And then just as quickly it came to a halt and a porter hopped out from one of the lead cars and placed a metal step on the ground. Further down the line, closer to us, another porter exited from his car. He grabbed Anna's bags for her as she turned to hug my father good-bye. She was crying.

"It's your life," he said. "Do what you want. Don't worry about your mother; she'll get over it."

She bent over and kissed me on the forehead and promised to write. It was a promise kept with diligence, a letter arriving monthly for the whole family, and every six months or so one specifically for me and Frank. I remember reading aloud the one where she explained the different vows she had to take and when she mentioned a vow of poverty, Frank laughed and said, "that one should be easy." I hadn't seen her since, and I had missed her.

———

"Wake up sleepy head," she said.

I opened my eyes and gazed up to a blurry black figure with white trim. I shut my eyes and opened them again. I had seen these outfits before at St. Anthony's and was, to a certain extent, accustomed to them, even though I never really quite understood their purpose. Looking up at what I now recognized as my sister, that purpose became very clear. Not only did the uniform define who they were, but, more importantly, to whom they belonged.

I sat up in bed. "When did you get here?"

"Last night, when you were asleep. Are you happy to see me?"

"You look different."

"It's still me."

"Do you have to wear that all the time?"

She rubbed my hair. "No, I don't. Mom's washing some clothes for me."

I tried to bring the sister I had always known into focus, to see beyond the habit and concentrate more on the face trapped within it. "You missed it. There was a huge fire yesterday."

"I know," she said, very concerned. "Mom told me about it."

Frank grunted in anger and pulled the covers over his head. Anna put a finger to her lips and I lowered my voice.

"Did she tell you Peter was on the roof?"

"No, she didn't. You can tell me all about it when you get up. Now, do I get a hug?"

We embraced. She had been gone three years but I had not forgotten her touch, or her smell, that squeaky clean blend of Prell shampoo and Ivory soap. "Ooh, I missed you guys so much." She put her hand on Frank's shoulder. "Both of you."

"I missed you, too," I said.

Frank slammed a pillow over his head. "I promise to miss you if you'll go downstairs"

"Get dressed and come on downstairs so mister grump can sleep. I'm making your favorite breakfast."

"Waffles?"

"Waffles."

"Alright!"

———

We sat together at the table, Anna and my mother pouring down the coffee, Mary and I working on a stack of waffles. I felt a little uncomfortable, thinking perhaps my mother would start in on Anna about being a nun, but aside from the occasional bit of sarcasm, the issue seemed to be settled.

"I thought you weren't coming until Christmas," said Mary.

"Well, I decided to come early so I could spend more time with all of you. That's okay, isn't it?"

"Oh, sure. I'm happy you're here."

"I met a really neat old man at the hospital who's gonna teach me how to pitch," I said.

"You did?" She looked to my mother for an explanation, as adults will do.

"Colored man..."

"He used to be in the Negro League," I said. "Did you know they had a league just for Negroes?"

"No, I didn't," said Anna. "What's the matter with him?" Again she looked to my mother.

"He has the big C," I said. "He's on the first floor, where they keep the really sick people, but I think he's gonna be okay."

"Well, I hope so," said Anna. Then she looked to my mother. "The big C?"

"Cancer," said my mother.

I felt a hand slap me gently in the back of the head. I knew it was Frank. Anna got up from the table.

"Well, it's about time you got up," she said and went to him, putting one arm around his shoulders.

"It's impossible to sleep around here."

"Oh, aren't you happy to see me?"

"Just as long as I don't have to go to church with you."

"Frank," said my mother, but without heat.

"That's okay. Maybe Michael will go."

"Maybe Martin," said Frank. "He doesn't know any better."

At this remark my mother rose from her chair, her eyes starting to glass over.

"That's not funny, young man."

"God, I'm just kidding."

"Mary, you and Michael do the dishes. I have work to do." She stomped out of the room.

"I'm not doing the dishes," I said.

"What's the matter with mom?" said Mary, ignoring my complaint.

"She's worried about Martin," said Anna. She gave Frank a little squeeze. "What are we going to do about your tongue?"

"What's wrong with it?"

"Oh, brother. Look, who wants to go shopping with me today?"

"I do!" said Mary.

"I promised Neely I'd be over today," I said.

"Who's Neely?"

"Cornelius. The old man. He's gonna show me some pitches."

"You better not waste any time then," said Frank. There was no irony in his voice whatsoever.

———

I decided to get in the second game of my World Series before going to see Cornelius; it was not going well. I put Koufax on the mound against Turley, a twenty-one game winner during the season who also pitched brilliantly during the real World Series. After seven innings, the Dodgers were down three-zip. Koufax had only given up three hits, but they all came in the fifth inning, coupled with his only walk, and an error by Jr. Gilliam (a rare occurrence indeed). Two of the three runs were unearned but there they were, nonetheless.

Norm Larker, who had had a decent first year with the Dodgers, opened up the inning pinch hitting for Koufax and promptly doubled to right field. Gilliam walked and Charlie Neal singled, loading the bases. (Not all singles were the same. Some allowed runners to advance one base, some, two. I could try and advance the runners two bases on a one-base single, but it required dipping into the stolen base sub-pile, a risk I was unprepared to take with no outs, three runs down, and the heart of the lineup coming to bat.)

Stengel went to the mound; it was the first trouble Turley had been in. Was he tiring? Gil Hodges stepped into the batter's box. I wanted Turley to stay. I liked the way the cards were going. But Stengel had other ideas. He waived his right arm and his ace right-hander, Ryne Duren, jogged in from the pen.

I gathered up the cards and prepared to shuffle them, but

first I wanted a peek at what might have been, promising myself I wouldn't let it affect my decision. The top card was a strike. I went on. Another strike. When I turned over the third card, I couldn't believe my eyes; it was a homerun. I sunk back into my pillow. Maybe Stengel wouldn't have pulled Turley. After all, he still had a three run lead and the Yankees had a one game advantage. And wouldn't it be beautiful, Gil Hodges, the quiet man, my hero, stepping in and hitting a grand slam.

I looked around the room, as if I were afraid someone might be watching, then I casually flipped Duren's card back into the bullpen and let the home run stand, vowing not to cheat again. There would still be five other games, and in fact there were still two innings left in this one. The Yankees could still win. I had rationalizations lined up for yards.

The Dodgers went on to win the game six-four (surprise), tying the series at one game each. The next three would be in L.A., and I would have started into number three but I was eager to get to the hospital and see Cornelius; and besides, the teams had to make that long trip out west to L.A.

The guilt associated with my indiscretion only lasted a few moments. After all, it was my game, my world. I had a right to control what happened, didn't I? There was just this one nagging question I couldn't quite answer. Then why play the game?

THIRTEEN

I stuck my head out Neely's doorway and checked the hall. All clear. I held the door open while he wheeled himself out and together we hurried toward the elevator, my glove and ball in his lap while I labored along behind, pushing his chair. A couple of patients made comments as we passed their rooms but I did not look over to respond. The reality of what was happening in those rooms was more than I wanted to absorb that morning, especially after Peter's close call with death. Today was my day to become a pitcher; everything else could wait.

We made it safely to the elevator and once inside I quickly pushed the button for the basement floor, and the doors pulled shut. Neely quietly inspected my glove. It was as worn as a baseball glove could be and literally falling apart, the lacing torn between the fingers, sloppy webbing and the pocket worn almost all the way through. It no longer even had the smell of leather. I had found it a couple of summers back in a trashcan at the park, brought it home and repaired it as best I could. Neely held it to his nose and then shook his head in disapproval.

"This thing looks older than me."

I shrugged my shoulders.

"Well, that's alright. Still got a few miles left on it."

The elevator doors opened. I wheeled Neely out into the

hall, pushed number three on the elevator and then hopped out, sending it up to the third floor to cover our tracks.

The hall ran about twenty feet to our left and maybe fifty to our right. I started to go left but Neely stopped me. "Other way."

"How do you know?"

"Gave myself a tour."

So we went right, all the way to the end where the hall turned again to the left for ten feet and then ended abruptly at a set of swinging doors, above which was a sign on the wall that read: MORGUE.

"Are we going in there?" I asked.

"Why not? It's quiet in there. You're not afraid, are you?"

"No, I, uh..."

"Good. It's the live ones you gotta worry about. Ain't nobody in there gonna bother you."

Neely pushed open the doors. I turned on the light, revealing a rather large, clean room with three very heavy looking tables—one of which held a covered object—a long counter with various pieces of medical equipment laid out, two large sinks and a couple of chairs. Against the far wall were two rows of what appeared to be rather large drawers. I did a quick count, eight total.

"Not so bad, is it?"

"Where are all the dead people?"

Neely pointed to the drawers. "Most of them are in those vaults, except for that one over there."

He pointed to the table with the sheet on it.

"Wanna look?"

"Not me! How come he's not put away?"

"Probably gonna open him up, see what killed him." He handed me the ball and then held my hand in his, inspecting

120

my grip. I kept glancing toward the body on the table.

"They can do that?"

"It's called an autopsy. But you just forget about him. He ain't going nowhere."

He grabbed for the ball but I instinctively tightened up on it.

"You got good hands. Maybe we can do something with you."

"Can you teach me to throw a curve?"

"One thing at a time. Boy your age can ruin an arm, he starts getting too cute. Now go on down there and show me what you got."

Neely squeezed the small, battered mitt onto his hand while I hurried past the vaults to the other end of the room. As I took my place he drew the mitt up just below his chin and pounded his fist into it, giving me my target. I took a full windup and—in an attempt to impress him—delivered a fastball, hard as I could possibly throw. It hit three feet in front of him and to his left but Neely just casually dropped the mitt to his left and snagged the wild pitch just off his knee.

"The idea is to get it here in the air," he said. "Try throwing a little easier."

He rolled the ball back to me (we only had one glove). I threw a dozen or so more; a couple pitches were pretty wild, but for the most part I stayed in the strike zone. Neely snagged them all, except one that was way over his head. It caromed off the back wall and smacked into the door of an empty vault, generating a piercing reverberation throughout the room. Neely retrieved the ball and wheeled himself down to my end of the room.

"You're changing your grip on every pitch."

"I am?"

"Here, let me show you. It's okay to try different ways of holding the ball—everybody's got their own way—as long as you're aware of what you're doing so you can figure out what works best for you."

He spun the ball around in his hand.

"Try it like this."

He wiggled his index finger in the air.

"Put your index finger and your middle finger across the wide seams, like so. Keep them about half an inch apart. Now, you want the stitches right under the pad of the fingers. See? Now these two fingers are gonna curl around the side of the ball, like so, and your thumb goes underneath. Got it?"

"I think so."

"You think so?"

"I mean, yes, sir. I got it."

"Okay, you try it."

He handed me the ball. I placed my index and middle finger across the seams and Neely gently pulled them apart. The smaller fingers naturally fell to the side but my hand was too small for my thumb to reach all the way under the ball.

"Okay, that's good. Now hand me the ball."

I gave it to him and he gave it right back.

"Now do it again."

We stood there for five minutes repeating the process time and again, Neely maintaining a calm steadfast approach throughout, as if these few minutes were as important to him as they were to me.

"Okay, now, we'll start with this grip for awhile. Later on you can experiment, change it around. The important thing is to start getting some consistent patterns, so eventually you'll know exactly what's working for you. Now, one other thing we should work on today is your delivery. Boys your age have a tendency to throw sidearm a little too much, but what you want is something closer to this."

Once again he took the ball away from me.

"This is what you're doing now," he said as he swung his arm out sidearm fashion. "This is what I want you to do, more out here, from behind the ear. Think of it as a clock. If your head is twelve o'clock, you're gonna want the ball to be in between there and two o'clock. One other thing; as you release the ball, snap your wrist like a whip."

The whip part I understood. I had seen Lash Larue every Saturday for the past month. The clock business caused me to go into a slight state of panic. My brain seemed to shut down. It was getting far too complicated for me. I had always thought you just picked up a ball and threw it, that some people were just born knowing how to do that and others never would. Now here Neely was, turning it into a science, making me think about every step. It seemed like homework, like school, and while I was excited to have him there giving his time and knowledge, I was frightened by the thought of the work ahead of me. He must have seen it in my eyes.

"Look, boy, most things worth doing take hard work. If they didn't, everybody'd be doing them. It ain't that bad. Now let's see you throw a few like this. Take your time, get your grip, think about your release before you go into your windup, see your hand pass your ear, see the ball leave your hand, and then forget about it, just throw the ball. Okay?"

"Okay."

He wheeled his chair back to the other end of the room. I gripped the ball, pictured it leaving my hand. I saw Lash, his purple horse up on his hind legs, the whip snapping through the air, snatching a gun out of some bandit's hand. I took my windup and delivered and the ball went way wide of Neely, crashing once again into the vault. My body felt awkward, uncoordinated. What had been a simple childish act of picking up a rock or a snowball and tossing it had now become a labor. I had no control. I began to question the wisdom of Neely's methods.

"Try it again," he yelled. "Look at my glove. See the ball hitting it."

Great. Just what I needed, something else to think about. I could feel my anger starting to rise. Once again I gripped the ball, saw the clock, the whip, imagined the ball entering the mitt, took my windup, delivered. Bamn! Once again it smacked against the vault, the sound reverberating around the room as if to say 'you missed, you missed, you missed'. Neely rolled the ball back to me but this time I just grabbed it, went into my windup and tossed it dead center into the mitt. The pop when it hit the leather was music to my ears.

Neely slowly wheeled himself across the room. He handed me the ball.

"If you're gonna throw the ball like that, you don't need me."

"I threw a strike."

"Even a broke clock tells the right time twice a day. That what you want?"

"But I don't understand, Neely. It feels too weird the other way."

"That's because it's new to you. You gotta make up your mind about something, boy. You can either trust me and work on the things I show you, or you can stick with your old ways. But you can't do both. Either way, don't make no difference to me, but don't be wasting my time if you ain't gonna do what I say..."

He glanced quickly toward the corpse and then back to me.

"...I don't have that much of it left."

"I'm sorry..."

"I don't care about no sorry stuff. Sorry don't change nothing'. This is for you, not me. If you don't want it, that's fine. I won't be angry with you. You're a good kid; I could tell that just watching you from my window. But you just have to decide what you want."

"Can I try it again?"

"I'm getting a little tired. Why don't you think on it for a spell and let me know what you decide."

I felt embarrassed. I wanted to say something but Neely reached over and put his hand on my shoulder and smiled.

"Don't worry about it," he said. "We all fight it at first. We all want to be wild and free; most times, that just ain't enough"

As we reached the door to leave I heard the elevator bell ring. I opened the door and walked quietly to where the hall turned, and looked down toward the elevator just in time to see the doors slide open and Ethel step out. She paused a few seconds, looked up and down the hall and then headed in our direction.

I ran back to Neely. "It's Ethel and she's coming our way." I reached up for the light switch but Neely grabbed my arm.

"Too late. She'll see the light go off."

He looked around the room.

"Come on."

I helped Neely into a closet but there was no room left for me.

"Get in one of the vaults," he said.

"What!"

"Go on, boy, hurry up." He grabbed a sheet from the shelf above his head. "Put this over you."

I checked a couple of vaults but they were occupied. I was tempted to look beneath the sheets—I had never seen a corpse—but I could hear Ethel's footsteps drawing nearer. I found an empty vault, pulled it open and hopped in. I did my best to close it from the inside and pulled the sheet over my body.

The door opened and Ethel came in, her heavy gait easy to follow as she moved closer. I noticed I didn't have the ball and mitt and wondered if they were with Neely. I could hear Ethel complaining aloud about the light being left on and those damn irresponsible doctors. Then, I felt the vault I was in move. She had closed it the rest of the way. The next few seconds seemed like hours as I imagined myself trapped inside, left for dead. For the first time in my short life I considered death and its loneliness. What if, when you die, you were aware of the darkness surrounding you? What if Peter was right and there wasn't a heaven, if we merely spent eternity in a little box six feet under the ground, alone, without our senses?

I began to hyperventilate and was about to scream when the vault opened up and the sheet was pulled back. There staring down at me, the blood all gone from her face, her mouth agape with the black horror that had filled my mind just seconds ago, stood Ethel. She sucked in a bunch of air and a scream momentarily stuck in her throat. She turned, released an ear piercing scream and ran out of the room.

I hopped out of the vault, happy to be back, and quickly helped Neely out of the closet. We took the second elevator up to the first floor and managed to sneak back into his room unnoticed. I helped him into his bed and then, hearing voices outside, quickly slid under the bed.

Ethel burst through the door. There was someone with her.

"Cornelius Brown!"

Neely was silent.

"He's asleep, Ethyl." I didn't recognize the second voice, a woman.

"I don't understand, he must have been with the boy..."

"Come on dear, you'll wake him up. You know how it is down there. Your mind can play tricks on you."

"But I saw him..."

"Come on, I'll get you a cup of coffee."

The door closed behind the two women and I slid out from under the bed.

"Boy, that was close. Neely."

I shook him gently and he opened his eyes, half asleep.

"Better run along boy, I'll see you tomorrow."

"Okay." I paused for a moment. "Neely?"

"Yeah." He was having a hard time keeping his eyes open.

"I was just wondering. When I first met you, you said you wondered when I was going to come and see you. Why did you pick me?"

He smiled. "I didn't pick you, son. I'd been waving to kids all week. You're the only one bothered to wave back. So I guess it was you who picked me."

"Oh. Neely...I'm gonna do it."

"What's that?"

"I'm gonna learn what you showed me."

"I know you will, boy."

I pulled back the blanket on his chair and grabbed the

mitt and ball. Neely looked over at me. "Tell your old man to get you a new glove." He closed his eyes.

"Sure, I'll tell him," I said and quietly left the room. All the way home I practiced my grip, and even fired off a couple of pitches at an occasional tree. I could do this thing, I thought, especially with Neely's help. I wondered what the chances were of getting a new mitt, and then I remembered my parent's conversation. It wasn't likely.

FOURTEEN

I built a snowman the next morning but rather than toss at the head, I formed another large block of snow and placed it in the catcher's position, drawing a circle in the strike zone as my target. The snow was perfect for packing, so constructing my batter and catcher was relatively easy.

First, the snowman. I started with a handful of firmly packed snow a little bigger than a baseball. At first I had to bear down on it to get it to pick up more snow but as it grew, my job got easier—not having to bend over and push—for the weight of the ball itself sucked up any snow in its path, sometimes going all the way down to bare earth. It made a crunching sound as I rolled it across the yard until at last its weight was too much for me and I brought it to rest. I formed another ball and set out again, this time ending with a smaller one that I could lift up and place atop the first, then another one smaller than the second for a head (I didn't bother with features) and finally another large ball for the squatting catcher.

Throughout the yard, a series of trails, different lengths and widths, crisscrossed one another as if a family of huge worms blindly searching for their home had at once converged and metamorphosed into a faceless ballplayer.

I had stayed out till dark the night before making snowballs, which had frozen overnight, producing—in size and weight—a reasonable facsimile to a hardball. I had to imagine the stitches but it was the best I could hope for, the alternative being throw my one baseball, retrieve it, and throw it again.

I had about one hundred balls and was determined to make each one count, running through Neely's instructions before each pitch: the grip; remember my ear—one o'clock; snap the ball; imagine the ball hitting the glove; don't throw too hard.

With each pitch I became more and more comfortable and with the comfort came control so that by the time I had used up half the balls, I was at least hitting the block of snow that held the target, or the snowman. And these were snowballs, frozen, yes, but still not as dense as the real thing, not nearly as easy to control.

"You're getting pretty good at that," said Anna as the screen door snapped shut behind her. She was out of her habit now and wearing some jeans and a sweatshirt. I had to do a double take.

"You look different," I said. It was the first time I'd seen her hair since she'd gone away. It was cut short like a boys; for comfort, I imagined.

She ran her fingers through her hair.

"Is it bad?"

"No, it's okay."

I reached down and picked up a snowball. "You wanna try one?"

"Oh, not me. I'll watch you."

I kneaded the ball.

"There's no face on your snowman."

"It's just a target."

I went into my windup and threw the ball but my concentration was broken and it went wild.

"I think I'm distracting you. Mom and I are going to the hospital to see Martin. I thought maybe you might want to go."

"I'll probably go over later," I said. "Isn't she working today?"

"No, she has the day off. Michael." She paused for a moment.

"What?"

"You know, Martin is very sick and there's a possibility... that is, sometimes..."

"Is he going to die?"

"Well, we don't know. We have to pray for him very hard and hope he's strong enough to get better, but I thought maybe you and I should talk about it."

As she talked, my eyes shifted back and forth from her to the target to the remaining snowballs on the ground. Some had begun to melt and it became apparent that shortly I would have one large formless pile of snow. I wanted to separate them and reform the ones that had suffered most from the warmth of the day. I didn't want to talk about Martin. I didn't want to think about death. I felt guilty for being so selfish and yet I couldn't control myself.

"I think he's gonna be alright," I said. "Is mom okay?"

"Mom is a very strong woman, but she is going to need all of our help right now."

"Sure."

I looked again to the snowballs.

"Well, if you need to talk later..."

"I'm okay. When do you have to go back?"

"I'm not sure. I'm not sure I am going back." She looked down at my pile of snowballs. "You better get back to your practice before your snowballs melt. I'll talk to you later."

She hugged me and then reached down and picked up a snowball and lobbed it gently toward the snowman. It only made it half way to the target.

"See. I told you," she said, and then hurried off into the house.

As I turned to face my target, Peter limped through the back gate and slowly made his way toward me. I quickly grabbed a snowball and tossed it at him.

"Hey, cut it out!"

"Sorry, I was trying to hit the snowman."

"Sure you were. What are you doing?"

"Practicing."

"Boring. Want to go to a movie?"

"Nope. How's your ankle?"

"It's okay. I had to go to the doctor this morning and get x-rays. My old man took me."

"In the morning?"

"Yeah. He thinks we're gonna get some money or something, on account of insurance. He was up early."

I picked up a snowball; it turned to mush and I grabbed one from the bottom of the pile—still firm—went through the ritual and tossed it. Strike.

"What's on?"

"The Creature Walks Among Us."

"I already saw it. They had some guy dressed up as the creature outside after the show got out."

"When was that?" said Peter, feeling cheated.

"Last week. He wasn't that scary, though. What's on at the Granada?"

"Oh, some grown-up movie. I think it's called The Tattered Dress, or something like that."

I stopped pitching.

"I saw a preview of it last week," he said "and they showed a woman's tit."

"They wouldn't do that."

"Well, they did. And I saw it."

Peter grabbed a snowball from the pile and tossed it haphazardly toward the target, missing by a couple of yards.

"You're such a liar," I said.

"I am not."

He limped over to a pile of wood by the nursery (he was really playing it up), grabbed a board and hobbled down to the snowman.

"What are you doing?"

"Bet you can't get one by me. Come on."

"How much?"

"Nickel."

I searched through the pile and picked the hardest one I could find, compressed it a bit to make it even harder, went into a wind-up and tossed a perfect strike right past him.

"Throw me another one!"

"Give me my nickel, first."

"Come on!"

"My arm's tired." I walked out toward Peter. He began poking at the snowman with his piece of wood.

"When you were up on the roof during the fire, did you think you were going to die?"

"I don't know. I don't think I thought much about it. There wasn't a lot of time to think."

"No, I guess not."

"So, how about it. You wanna go to the movies?"

"Think we could sneak in?" I asked.

"Sure. My cousin's working today. I thought you already saw it?"

"I mean the Granada?"

"Oh, I don't know. I think you have to be eighteen."

"Did you really see her tit?"

"Yeah, and it was big, too."

"I saw my sister's once."

"That doesn't count," he said and then he swung the stick at the snowman's head and it exploded into a million tiny snowflakes that slowly drifted to the ground.

FIFTEEN

"Lots of folks think Satchel Paige was the best pitcher, but for my money, I'd have to say it was Smokey Joe Williams. I remember one game, I'd just joined the Giants—think it was 1917—anyway, Ol' Smokey struck out twenty men. Twenty men! Why, there ain't but twenty-seven outs in an entire game. Funny part is, he lost the game one to nothing on account of an error. Well, that's baseball."

I sat on the cold cement floor, my back against the steel vaults, working my way through a peanut butter sandwich. The body from our previous visit had been removed from the table.

"I'm not saying Satchel wasn't great—he was—it's just sometimes I think people bring him up because he eventually played in the majors, so they were more familiar with him, you know."

"How come Smokey Joe didn't make it to the majors?"

"Well, because, he was too old by the time they started letting black folks in."

"I'll bet he was pretty mad, huh?"

"Well, son, that's hard to say. Didn't really know the man, personally. Maybe he was. Lot of fellows were pretty upset. If a man is good at what he does, he ought to have a chance to prove himself. But it doesn't always work out that way in this world and it doesn't do anybody no good going around full of anger at everybody and everything."

His voice had begun to rise at this point and he paused for a second before he continued.

"There are some things in this world only time can change. We had a lot of great days playing in the Negro Leagues. Can't nobody take that away. And we beat plenty of Major League teams. We had the ability and we knew it. Lot of white players knew it too."

"Do you think you could have made it to the majors?"

"Well, there's those say I could have. I wasn't no Smokey Joe, mind you, but I had a few tricks up my sleeve. Pitched three perfect innings once against Dizzy Dean's all-stars. See, they had to call themselves 'all-stars' 'cause the commissioner wouldn't allow them to wear their team uniforms when they were playing against the black teams. Wouldn't look right, you know, bunch a colored boys whippin' the New York Yankees, or Brooklyn Dodgers. Yes sir, that was something. And I was forty years old by then. That was my last year."

Neely took a swig of his Pepsi and held the bottle out in front of him as if it were some sort of icon to which he then paid homage to with a loud burp.

"That's better. I'm not supposed to drink these, you know. Sugar problem. Can't see how it matters much, now. You know, when you get to L.A., you'll have a lot more time to practice. Sun's out year-round out there."

"I don't know if we're going. I don't think my dad wants to. Neely, do you think I might be good enough to be a real ballplayer when I grow up?"

"You're already a real ballplayer."

"You know what I mean."

Neely shook his head. "Now, why is it everybody always wants to know about tomorrow? Did you know tomorrow never comes, 'cause as soon as it gets here, it's today."

I sat very still, staring up at Neely, waiting patiently for an answer.

"That's not what you want to hear, is it? Truth is, boy, I don't know. I can tell you this: It takes a lot more than knowing how to throw a baseball to be a professional."

"What do you mean?"

"There's plenty of guys walking around with the talent who don't have the discipline. They're the guys who won't show up for practice, or neglect their health, or maybe they're just afraid."

"Of what?"

"Afraid of the work, maybe. Afraid they might fail. Or even worse, afraid they might succeed. Some men are more comfortable with failure than success. But the way I see it, if you want something bad enough and you try as hard as you can, then you never lose. Your part is to be the best ballplayer you can be. That's the part you have some control over; and remember why you started playing the game in the first place—because it's fun. Maybe you'll make the team, maybe you won't. Maybe you'll find something else you like better someday..."

"Better than baseball?"

"Well, now, you never know. Point I'm trying to make is, whatever you do, do it well and try not to worry about all the rest of that stuff."

"My dad says only one in a million can make it to the big leagues. Says it's a waste of time."

"You're not hearing what I'm telling you, are you boy? Look, if you're thinking about a Mickey Mantle or Willie Mays, well, I suppose those guys are one in a million, maybe one in ten million. They have a special gift. Now, most of us, no matter how hard we try, we ain't ever going to reach that level of ability, but what we can do is work on what we got. That's what most your Major League players do, and that's what all of us have to do, whether it's baseball or anything else.

"I don't mean to say nothing bad about your father, but, far as I'm concerned, doing what you love ain't never a waste of time. Now, I'm sorry to hear he feels that way about it. Maybe he had some special thing he liked doing, something close to him that didn't work out like maybe he thought it would."

"I don't think so."

"You ever ask him?"

"No. I don't really talk to him much. He just mostly works. He drives a cab. But I don't think he likes it very much."

"I think we can rule out cab driver as his dream job. But sometimes a man's gotta put the food on the table. Easy to get lost doing that, and forget all about your dreams. But he's all grown up now and that's for him to figure out. If it's making him unhappy that's a sad thing, but it belongs to him—not you. Fact is, most of us never get to live our dream. Just the way life is. But even when your dream falls away, you still have a life you have to live. That's when we find out what we're made of."

'I'm not sure I know what you mean."

Neely took another long swig of his soda, set the bottle down and stared off for a minute before he started in again.

"Knew a fellow once, good ball player around thirty years old, had been in the League for a good ten years. He met a woman and she wanted him to marry her and settle down, get a regular job. But this fellow, he was certain the Major

League was going to start letting Negroes in at any time so he told this gal he wanted her to give him one more year and if things didn't work out he would quit and they would get married. This was in the late twenties.

"What happened?'

"Well, a year came and went and nothing changed, so he asked her for another year and she said okay."

"She sounds like a nice lady."

Neely had a look on his face like he was far away. "She was the finest, I can tell you that."

Another long silent spell. "So, did they get married?"

His voice got very quiet. "The second year was up and this fellow struggled with his decision. A couple of months went by and one day he woke up and everything seemed clear to him. The Major Leagues were never gonna let any of us in, least wise not while we were still young. He sat down and wrote a letter to let his girl know he was ready. Funny thing is, that very day, before he even mailed his letter, he got one from her saying she couldn't wait anymore and maybe it was better she didn't try and pull him away from something he loved so much. She was engaged to marry another man."

"What happened?"

"Well, this is what I'm talking about. He lost his dream and his woman at the same time and now he had to face the future. He felt like a fool, like he had been chasing a fool's dream and it had cost him a chance for a good life with this woman. He spent the next four months…well let's just say, his behavior was less than stellar, till one day he woke up and realized he still had a life to live, and he had to decide what kind of life that was gonna be. It's like that Shakespeare fellow wrote: 'to be or not to be.' He put away all thoughts of the Majors and set out to do what he did best: play baseball.

You understand what I'm trying to tell you?"

"Maybe. I don't know." All this talk about my dad and dreams that don't come true was making me uncomfortable. I changed direction. "You ever meet Jackie Robinson?"

———

I spent the rest of the afternoon there in the morgue with Neely, practicing my pitching and taking breaks to listen to his tales of the glory days of the Negro Leagues, the greats like Cool Papa Bell, perhaps the fastest man to ever play ball. "Faster than Ty Cobb, no doubt about it. He was so fast he could hit the light switch on the wall and be under the covers before the light went out."

Or Biz Mackey, who taught Roy Campanella. Bill Drake, who used to sandpaper the ball to give it more break. Oscar Charleston. "Best all around ball player ever lived," said Neely.

He had seen them all and played with or against the best, barnstorming through the mid-west, pitching tents, playing ball during the day, fishing in the evening. He had played in the first Black World Series in 1924 and enjoyed some fairly lucrative years throughout that decade. But with the depression, hard times befell the league. Instead of traveling in comfort via the Pullmans, players had to settle for the bus. The money dwindled. Winter leagues in Florida and Cuba folded. It became apparent to players like Neely, approaching middle age, that it was time to move on.

He was eager to recall his glory days of baseball, but his life beyond that was somewhat of a mystery. He had never married or had any children. After his playing career ended, he coached for a few years and did some scouting, but there just weren't many jobs available. Once the majors opened up to blacks, the Negro League completely fell apart, leaving hundreds of men like Neely, past fifty, without skills, with no place to go. He drifted from one menial job to another, managing to keep himself clothed and fed. I tried to press him for details but he brushed me aside.

"Listen, son. I started playin' baseball when I was nine years old and quit when I was forty. Everything before and after that don't add up to much and it certainly won't help you learn how to pitch. We're on a limited time schedule here; no point using it up talking about me. You wanna throw a few more before we leave?"

"Sure." I ran down to the other end of the room. I didn't even have to look at my grip to get it right; I could feel the seams in place and they felt good. I took a full wind-up and delivered a fastball, letter high for a strike.

SIXTEEN

I came down with a cold and with Martin fighting pneumonia there was no way my mother would let me out of the house. It was the perfect time to move along with the Series.

The weather in L.A. was perfect for baseball, a pleasant seventy-two degrees—shirtsleeve weather. Johnny Padres got the nod for game three and Don Larsen went for the Yankees.

There was something about Johnny Padres that never quite set right with me. He seemed to constantly be in trouble on the mound, even in the games he won. And lying there at night listening to my transistor, I could always sense it coming. Usually it was a control problem; he'd start hanging his change-up or his fast ball would begin to rise and before you knew it there would be two or three walks, or somebody would get hold of one of those changes and hit it out. So I have to be honest and say I really didn't want to have him start, but it was his turn and I figured I owed him a chance. But I had my mind made up to pull him at the first sign of trouble.

Well, there was no trouble. He pitched the closest thing to a perfect game so far in my league. Only two Yankees reached first base: Bill Skowron, on an error in the sixth, and Hank Bauer on a single. That was it. I felt a little bad for Larsen, for he pitched a good game, giving up only seven hits and two runs in seven innings. Duren came in to relieve him and the Dodgers picked up four more off him in one inning and went on to win it, six-zip.

Drysdale won game four against Whitey Ford and it looked like maybe L.A. would take it in five, but Koufax got hammered in the fifth game, twelve-two, setting the scene for the final two games in New York.

I spent most of Thursday getting the players' stats up to date so that by Friday I had pretty much had my fill of baseball and was ready to get outside again. My mother, having taken my temperature and gazed down my throat, decided it was okay for me to brave the great outdoors but that if I were planning on visiting Cornelius I should wait another day, just to be on the safe side—for his sake.

Anna offered to take me Christmas shopping and I accepted. I hadn't been to town since the day of the fire and was interested in seeing what, if any, new toys had come in. It was, I believe, my first experience shopping with a woman.

She wanted to get my mother a new scarf. Did I like the blue one with the yellow flowers or the plain green? Or what about this one here, with the poka-dots? Oh, this is nice, what do you think of this? And on and on. She even tried to get me to model a couple for her!

We stopped at Hill's Drugstore for lunch and she bought me a root beer float and grilled cheese sandwich. The counter was full so we took one of the wood booths along the back wall. There were a few places in town that made root beer floats, but Hill's made the best. They poured the root beer from a keg into an icy cold mug, and then added the ice cream to it, which helped keep the foam to a minimum. Absolutely the best!

Anna had settled on the blue scarf with the tiny yellow flowers and as we sat and ate our lunch she occasionally opened the box and stared at it as if she were suffering from buyer's remorse. She would cock her head and open her mouth to speak but I would quickly look away, leaving her words suspended just that side of her lips.

Finally, she got it in. "I hope she likes it."

I was sucking air through my straw, a little foam all that remained of my float.

"She likes these colors," she continued and I pushed the empty glass away from me and looked her way.

"Why aren't you going back?"

"Back where?"

"To the convent. You said you might not go back."

"Oh. Well, I'm not sure." She had pulled the scarf from the box and was staring at it now as if in a trance.

"I thought once you joined you couldn't quit."

"Well, not exactly. It's something you shouldn't take lightly, but no one forces you to stay." Her voice began to trail off. "Sometimes things happen..."

"What happened?"

"It's so beautiful."

"Anna."

She refolded the scarf and returned it to the box.

"What happened?"

She smiled. It was a smile reserved for mothers and their small children. It seemed like I was getting a lot of that lately and I was finding it a little irritating.

"I'm not really sure," she said, almost in a whisper. "Nothing in particular, really. I'm just not sure it's what I really want." Then, as if someone had waved a wand over us, the spell was broken. She reached into her purse for a cigarette, lit it, and in her normal, jovial voice added, "We better get going if we want to finish our shopping."

There weren't any new mitts in the toy store window but Mr. Allen saw me through the glass and waved us inside. He was an older man, maybe in his sixties, with a back shaped like a comma, reducing his height to just a few inches taller than me. He had been an athlete when young, played college ball and even coached for awhile, but his arthritis had guided him to a more docile profession of running a store. He had told me these things during my numerous trips to his store, but never with a hint of regret or disappointment in his voice. I rather liked him.

"I have something here you might care to look at, Michael," he said as he pulled a box out from under the counter. "Just came in today."

I tore open the box and the smell of the leather floated out like the breath of angels.

"It's a new Wilson! Is this an A-2000?"

"Yes. It's a new model. The same one Don Drysdale uses," he said.

"No, he wears a Spalding," I said.

"I don't think so. But, what do I know; I only sell them."

I pounded my fist repeatedly into the pocket. The glove was a little big for my hand but I thought perhaps by summer I could get used to it.

"How much does a glove like that cost?" asked Anna.

"This is a very nice glove," said Mr. Allen. "Genuine cowhide. Very nice glove."

"It is very nice," said Anna and she lit a cigarette. "How much is it?"

"Well, a glove like this in Chicago would be seventeen, maybe eighteen dollars." He lifted the bifocals that hung at his chest and placed them on the tip of his nose—as if he were going to read some fine print—and closely inspected the box.

As far as I could tell, there wasn't much writing on it other than the word, Wilson. "I could probably sell it for fifteen."

He may as well have said fifteen hundred.

"Did you get very many?" I asked.

He set the box down but kept the glasses on, peering over the top of them as he spoke. "I got three of these and two of the Johnny Padres signature model. But of course, the Johnny Padres ones are for southpaws."

"Oh, what's a southpaw?" asked Anna

Mr. Allen and I looked at each other, shook our head and answered in unison. "It's a left-hander."

"Oh."

I took the glove from my hand and set it back in the box. "Thanks a lot for letting me see it."

"A glove like this, I won't have for long," he said.

"Thank you," said Anna and we left the store.

We stopped in front of the store as Anna retrieved a fresh cigarette from her purse. Mr. Allen set the new glove up on display in the window and placed a fifteen-dollar tag in the pocket. A boy about my age, and a man loaded down with packages, stopped in front of the window. The boy pointed toward the glove and the man smiled and nodded yes, checked his watch, then ushered the boy along.

"That's a pretty nice glove, huh?" said Anna.

"Yeah. I like the Spalding, like Drysdale uses, but that one's pretty nice, too. He won seventeen games year before last."

"Who?"

"Don Drysdale."

"Oh. Of course," she said. "And he is…?"

I glanced over in astonishment. Anna could recite the Ten Commandments, name a couple hundred saints and tell you when they were canonized or explain in detail all the sacraments, but she had no idea who Don Drysdale was. Our worlds were so far apart, and I suspected they would grow even more distant as time went on.

"It's not important," I said.

We moved slowly down Main Street, weaving our way through the crowd of shoppers, their arms full of colorful packages. I imagined them all delivering their loads at my feet, the pile growing bigger and bigger until at last I was surrounded by presents. I would have to open my way to the outside world.

As we came around the corner I was roused from my fantasy by the musty smell of smoldering ash from where once had stood the Murray Building. What little of the brick walls that had survived had since been razed with a wrecking ball; a rope now stretched across the front of the lot with 'keep out' signs attached every few feet. A few wreaths had been tied to the rope in memory of those who had perished.

"Maybe you should write a letter to Santa."

There it was again. "Anna. I'm not a little kid, you know."

"Oh, well. My mistake. Maybe when you say your prayers you could make a special request. You're not too old to pray, are you?"

"No, I guess not." I considered asking her if she thought the people who had died in the fire had been praying for God to help them, but I really didn't want to talk about praying or the glove. I wanted to bury the thought of it as soon as possible.

"Do you think it would be alright if Neely came over for Christmas?"

"Oh, I don't know, Michael. Better let me talk to mom about it. Do you think the hospital will let him out?"

"I just wanted everyone to meet him."

"I know you do and we'd all like to meet him. Tell you what. Why don't you make him a present and on Christmas morning you and I and whoever else wants to come along will go and visit him at the hospital. Would you like that?"

"Yeah. That would be great. You'll like Neely. He's real funny most of the time and he knows just about everything about pitching. I'm learning a lot."

"Well, then, we should make him something special."

"What do old people like?"

Anna laughed. "They like the same things as young people, just as long as it's from the heart."

I made a snowball and tossed it at one of the 'keep out' signs. The impact sent a shudder throughout the length of the rope and powder broke loose from the wreaths. If only I had fifteen dollars.

SEVENTEEN

It was getting close to dinnertime when we arrived home. Anna had gotten tired out walking around town so she called for a taxi to bring us back, hoping that perhaps my father would be available. As it turned out, he was making a run out to Pontiac, so we had to ride with one of the other drivers, a man named Bill who was my father's age and someone I had previously met; in fact, I had met most of the drivers in town. My father had told all of us if we were ever stuck and needed a ride home we could always walk to the station and someone would give us a ride. Bill recognized us and was good enough to turn the meter off for our short trip home, but Anna insisted he accept a tip. (He wasn't that hard to convince.)

The smell of pine needles hit us the minute we opened the door, as did Mary's voice.

"They're back, they're back. Can we start now?"

"Well, look at that," said Anna.

"We got a tree!"

They had set it up in a metal stand in the corner of the living room. It was a tall Noble, maybe six feet—which was tall in our house—a little thin in a few places but, all in all, not bad looking. Mary and Carol had gotten out all the ornaments and lights from the cellar, and Carol sat now on the floor, testing the various strands of lights and replacing any burned out bulbs.

"How was your shopping?"

Anna set her packages on the couch and took off her coat. "It's cold out there. Starting to snow. But we had a good time, didn't we Michael?"

"Sure," I said. I took off my jacket and gloves and hurried over to the tree. "I get to do the lights. Where's Frank?"

"He went sledding," said Mary.

I pulled off my boots and tossed them toward the dining room.

"When did this get here?"

"Dad got it," said Mary.

"You better get those boots out of here before mom sees them," added Carol.

"Well, this is great," said Anna. "I'll make some popcorn to string."

I started to get up but Anna grabbed my boots for me on her way out. Mary and I dug into the ornaments, eager to get started.

"I want to do that one."

"I just got here. I want to."

"If you two are going to argue, neither one of you are going to help."

"Yeah, stop arguing," said Mary. "Why don't you go ride your sled with Frank."

"Maybe I don't want to."

Mary and I removed the bulbs from the boxes and separated them into piles by color, the solid blues, reds and golds (those with a smooth finish), into one, and solid colors with a matte finish and those with snow-caps that dripped down the sides, into another. There were also a few silver ones that would show your reflection in them, but all distorted like a fish eye lens on a camera. And there were others covered with material with tiny particles of silver glitter glued on that shot small beams of reflected light about the room. We had a special pile for those without hooks, which we left for Carol to fix after she finished with the lights.

My mother came down the stairs carrying a small Nativity scene, complete with plaster of Paris figurines, and a white sheet.

"Oh, good, you found it," said Carol.

She set it down by the tree and handed the sheet to Mary, who then unfolded it and wrapped it around the base of the tree, which both hid the stand and created the illusion of snow on the ground. I picked through the Nativity pieces. Everything seemed to be there but one of the three wise men was missing his head. I dug through the straw but was unable to find it. An image of Frank tossing it against a wall passed quickly through my head. I paused and attempted to recollect if that event had actually occurred but I couldn't pin it down to an actual memory, or just a random thought, so I quickly let it go.

Everything was covered with dust so I unbuttoned the sleeve of my shirt and began wiping clean the individual pieces. Carol said she'd get a can of spray-on snow from the dime store later on to replace that which had worn off the roof.

"Carol, I need to go over to Phoebie's to help her get ready for the party. Will you drive me?"

"Alright. You guys can finish putting hooks on these bulbs while I'm gone. But be careful not to break anything." She ran upstairs for her coat and my mother got one from the living room closet.

I could hear the popcorn begin to pop in the kitchen. Anna came into the living room and Carol returned with her coat.

"Where you going?"

"I'm taking mom over to Phoebie's. I'll be right back."

"We'll wait for you to do the tree."

Mary and I grumbled a little when we heard that, but I was actually more concerned about the popcorn.

Anna turned to my mother. "How's Martin?"

My mother drew in a deep breath. "I just talked to Doctor Fowley a few minutes ago. He says he's stable."

Her voice sounded weak to me and I looked up at her. She seemed tired and distant, not at all herself. Despite a shortage of money and a houseful of children, my mother was usually a person of good humor with more energy than someone half her age. She had her imperfections and prejudices but overall, she was easy to live with. Which is not to say she was not an emotional person. She could cry on a dime—and often did—and did not hesitate to yell at us if we got under her skin, but hers was a controlled response to the day-to-day irritants. There were no unexplained explosions—one did not tiptoe around her—but rather, if you could put a meter on emotional responses from one to ten, she would always be hovering somewhere between three and seven, whereas my father was capable of going from a one to a ten in a heart beat. So seeing her today in such a quiet somber mood, while unusual, did not in any way signal something far worse just around the corner. I took great comfort in this as a child, and if I have any emotional stability as an adult, I give all credit for it to her.

"Mom, why don't you stay here and rest," said Anna. "I can go and help Phoebie."

"No, you stay here with the kids. I need to get out of the house for a while. Do me good."

"Popcorn's burning," I said.

"Oh, my God," said Anna, and she darted back toward the kitchen.

———

Frank came in about an hour later. We were pretty much finished with the tree. It looked great. Most of the lights still worked and there were plenty of bulbs to fill in the thin spots. Carol had stopped at the store on her way back from Phoebie's and picked up some icicles. We put on a ton of those and Anna was just about ready to wrap the popcorn—what little had survived—that she had strung.

"Frank, look, we got a tree."

"No kidding."

"We would have waited for you," said Anna, "but we didn't think you cared much about it."

"Doesn't matter. What's the deal, anyway? Christmas coming early this year?"

"Very funny," said Carol.

"We did save one thing for you, though," said Anna.

She pulled an angel out of the box and handed it to Frank. It was about as beat up as an angel can get, I imagine, but it still had a halo and that was good enough for us.

"We're all too short."

"Ever hear of a ladder?"

"Guess we just needed a man to think of that," said Anna.

"I thought of it," said Mary.

"Congratulations," said Frank

She stuck out her tongue but he ignored her. He reached up to the top of the tree and stuck the angel on. It leaned slightly to one side.

"That's one tired angel."

Anna put her arm around Frank. "Just three days till

Christmas, Mr. Scrooge."

Frank smiled. "Bah, humbug."

———

Anna was the first to put presents under the tree. She had wrapped mine in white paper with little Santa Clauses printed on it. There was one for everybody. Mary's was wrapped with paper identical to mine and the rest were in a solid red foil with white ribbons around them. I held mine up to the light, shook it, toyed with the tape in hopes it might accidentally come loose—no such luck—and even considered ripping away a small corner of the paper, thinking I might get a little information from the box, but decided against it. One thing I was sure of: it wasn't a glove. She had gotten Mary a pair of pajamas and my box was shaped the same and was light, so I figured it was pajamas for me, too.

"You want me to tell you what you got?" I asked Mary.

"No! I want it to be a surprise." But she was shaking hers, too.

The smell of Anna's freshly baked garlic toast brought a growl to my stomach. We'd been so busy with the tree I'd forgotten all about food. My dad had come downstairs earlier and passed through the room like a thief, with only the creak of the bottom step betraying his arrival. He was busy now in the kitchen, heating up a batch of Chicken soup my mother had prepared.

"Time to eat," he called out from the other room. I gave my present one final shake then set it back down below the tree. Maybe later I would solve the puzzle.

My mother arrived back from Phoebie's just as we were sitting down to eat. The wind snatched the porch door from her hand and slammed it against the wall so hard we all jumped from our seats.

"Jesus Christ!" said my dad, and I heard my mom close the door behind her.

"Sorry!"

Outside, the car backed down the drive and pulled away from the house. When my mother entered the dining room, she was covered with snow. She took off her scarf and wiped her face. A small puddle formed around her boots.

"It's really coming down out there."

"Where's Carol going?" asked my dad.

"Over to Richard's." She moved to the register and pulled off her boots. "I told her she could use the car."

"Well, you might have asked me first. What if I was planning on going somewhere? She shouldn't be driving in this weather, anyway."

My mother took off her coat and laid it over a chair.

"She's a good driver, and if you need the car, just call her up and tell her. Where were you planning on going, anyway?"

"I'm not. That's not the point."

"Well, what is the point, Sam?"

Mary and I looked at each other in anticipation. Anna jumped in.

"This soup is going to get cold if we don't eat. Mom, sit down, I'll get you a bowl."

"Where's Frank?" said my dad.

"He's downstairs with Kelly," I said.

"Well, go tell him it's time to eat."

I started to get up from my seat, but just then Frank burst into the room.

"Mom, Kelly's having her puppies!"

My mother took a deep breath. "Oh, boy. Get a bucket of warm water and some towels."

I jumped up from my seat. "I'm coming, too."

"Me, too," said Mary.

"The two of you can sit right back down there and finish your dinner. You can come down later."

"Do you need some help?" asked Anna.

"Frank and I can handle it."

I started to complain but my father cut me off before I could finish my sentence.

"You heard your mother. Eat."

———

By the time I got downstairs, three of the pups had already been delivered. They lay motionless in a cardboard box, their lifeless bodies no bigger than three small mice. Frank was close to tears.

"They're not moving," I said.

Frank just glared at me.

"What's wrong with them?"

"They're stillborn, Michael," said my mom, gently stroking the back of Kelly's neck.

"What's that?"

"We should have had her fixed," said Frank, mostly to himself. "She's too old."

"Here comes another one," said my mother.

"What's stillborn?" I repeated.

"Dead," said Frank. "Born dead."

The fourth one was born alive. It was as black as the coal in the next room, its fur short and shiny, its tiny eyes sealed shut. My mother placed it at one of Kelly's teats and it began to feed. Three more came shortly thereafter, two white ones and one black with a white neck and feet. They were still living when Mary arrived.

"Did she have them?"

"She's all through," said my mother, who then flipped the lid over the box, got up from the floor and wiped her hands on a towel.

"Let me see," said Mary. She bent down to Kelly. "Oh, they're so sweet."

Frank grabbed the box.

"What's in there?" asked Mary.

"Nothing," said Frank. Mary turned her attention to the pups and Frank grabbed the shovel by the coal bin and followed my mother up the stairs.

———

I woke up in the middle of the night sweating under my blankets and pushed them off me. (It was the warmest winter night in that house that I can remember.) Frank had yet to come to bed and I figured he was still in the cellar with Kelly and the pups. I considered going down there but quickly drifted back to sleep.

I went down first thing the next morning and found him asleep on a piece of old carpet. There were three more dead pups. I woke Frank and went outside with him to bury them in the corner of the yard. The ground was pretty hard but they were so little we only had to dig about six inches deep to cover them. We stood there in our shirtsleeves, oblivious to the cold as a light snow slowly covered the newly dug grave. Frank wiped the tears from his eyes and picked up the shovel. "Let's go in," he said.

Only one of the pups survived. Frank named him Sport.

EIGHTEEN

Neely was bundled up in his wheelchair, gazing out the window, when I came in. I was still feeling bad about the pups. I kept seeing their tiny, lifeless bodies snuggled together in the hole Frank had dug that morning.

"That's quite a storm out there," he said. Thought maybe you wouldn't make it today."

There was something in his voice today, or was it something that was missing from it. His words were slow and deliberate, as though his mind were on something else. He had yet to turn and look my way.

"Sorry I'm late. I was up late last night."

"I didn't get much sleep, myself," he said, finally turning from the window. "You didn't bring your glove?"

"I can't stay today."

There was a moment of silence.

"Come on over here, boy."

I walked over to Neely and we both stared out the window at the driving snow, coming down harder now—it seemed to fall in sheets—so that we could see only a few feet beyond the window. Nothing but white sheets of cold snow and a blurry image of distant trees. I felt drawn to it and yet somehow threatened by it at the same time, as though some heretofore unrecognized danger had suddenly revealed itself to me, a danger whose essence I didn't quite understand.

"What do you see out there?"

"I don't know. Snow...some trees."

"What else?"

"I can't see anything else. It's snowing too hard."

"Look closer."

I stared intently out the window. It was all a white blur.

I searched the shadowy branches for signs of life but there was nothing. The squirrels had all taken shelter, and if there were blue jays, they were hiding. The more I stared, the less I saw, until finally everything disappeared, everything but our images reflecting back in the glass.

"I see our reflection in the window."

Neely laughed out loud. "And ain't that a beautiful thing to see," he said. "A beautiful thing. Yes sir, it's great to be alive. Long as you can see that reflection, you're doing okay. Look straight at it and don't be afraid."

I stared at myself for a few seconds, totally confused, then turned away to look at Neely, who reached over and patted me on the head.

"Now," he said, his mood having lifted abruptly, "what's bothering you today?"

I had almost forgotten.

"It's nothing."

Neely turned from the window. "Don't look like nothin'."

"Kelly had her pups last night."

"Well, now, that's good news. How many did she have?"

"Seven."

"Seven. That's a good size litter. I had me a bit...a dog, once, had herself eleven pups."

I walked away from the window and sat on the edge of Neely's bed. "There's only one left."

"Oh, I see."

"I helped Frank bury them this morning. They were so little. Neely, why does everything have to die?"

I could feel the tears pushing their way out. I fought hard to hold them back. The storm grew more intense so that even the outline of the trees disappeared, as though someone had pulled a huge white blanket over the hospital. The air inside grew thick.

"Death is out there, that's for sure. And it's scary, I think, because there ain't nobody around can tell us about it. Not like anything else. We all gotta do it ourselves, kinda like being born. You understand? But it must be the right thing to do; everybody and everything's gonna do it. We're gonna close our eyes and lay back and see what happens next. Maybe we'll just start all over again. That wouldn't be so bad, would it? Or maybe we won't. Now, if that's the case, seems to me we best be appreciating the time we have."

"But Kelly's puppies didn't get any time."

"I know. I know, that don't seem fair, does it?"

The tears had found their way out by now, silently.

"Go ahead and cry, boy. Ain't nothin' wrong with that. Hurts to lose someone. Supposed to. Feel the hurt and never forget it."

He was no longer looking at me, but had turned his attention once again to the falling snow. He spoke softly.

"That way, when someone new comes into our lives, maybe we'll treat them a little bit better, appreciate them a little more. That's something you're never too young to learn. Or too old."

He turned back toward me. "So you go on and cry now. Cry for those pups; let 'em know how much they meant to you."

I wiped my face with my sleeve. "Are you going to die soon?"

"I don't know, Michael. I suspect it won't be long."

I got up from the bed and returned to Neely's side.

"I don't want you to," I said and threw my arms around him and let it all out. I could barely feel his arms as he wrapped them around me, yet I still felt safe within them, and as he struggled to hold them up I prayed he would live forever, that time would slow down, that God would make an exception to the rule.

"Are you afraid?" I asked.

Neely moved his hands to my shoulders and gently pushed me back. "Afraid of death? I won't lie to you, son. I'm a little scared. It's only natural. You were afraid to change your grip on the ball, but you did it anyway. Every one has fears. It's how you face them that matters. Now, if I'm not mistaken, you saw two reflections in that window. I ain't dead yet."

He reached up and brushed away my tears with his pajama sleeve. "Let's cheer up around here. It's almost Christmas."

"We're going to a party Christmas Eve. I wish you could come."

"That's too much excitement for this old body. You can tell me all about it."

I began to feel a little better. "I will. I have a present for you, too. And my sister said she'd come with me to meet you."

"Well, that sounds great. Things are looking up around here."

As the snow let up, I could begin to make out a few kids with their sleds at the top of the hill. I wanted to join them and yet it seemed strange to me that I could have felt so badly just moments ago. Nothing had changed—the puppies were still dead; Neely was dying; Martin was sick—and yet I felt better. Not that I—like everyone—hadn't gone through quick mood changes before. I had just never given them much thought, never tried to understand them. These thoughts brought with them an uneasiness, a feeling that I was venturing into new territory, a terrain both frightening, yet somehow liberating. What was this strange phenomenon and where would it take me? I felt suddenly very vulnerable.

"I got an idea. It's still early. Why don't you go home and get your glove. You ain't gonna learn how to throw a curve ball hanging around here worrying about people dying."

"Really! You'll show me?"

"I think you're about ready."

We said our good-byes and I hurried out of the room, forgetting, for the moment, these new thoughts. I felt a terrific lightness about me, and it was good.

In fact, I felt so good, so light, I seemed to float down the corridor—oblivious to the sickness around me—and through the reception area, the busy sounds and chatter blending to a high pitch like a chorus of angels cheering me on.

I grabbed my sled, pushed through the doors into the cold air, took a running start and tossed my sled down into the snow. I was on my way!

But in my reverie, I hadn't noticed the two figures up ahead of me, not until it was too late. It was Thornton and his buddy, directly in my path. I tried to steer around them but Thornton stepped quickly to his left, forcing me into a bank of snow. I came to a dead stop.

"Well, look who's here," said Thornton. "Where's big brother today?"

I jumped up from my sled.

"Let's pants him," said his friend.

"I didn't do nothing to you," I said.

"Yeah, well, that ain't the way it works, squirt."

I tried to make a run through the middle of them but Thornton grabbed me by the arm and spun me around. Then he stuck his leg behind mine and pushed me backward and I crashed down hard on my back. Before I knew it, he was on top of me, pinning my shoulders to the ground with his knees. I thrashed about, trying to free myself but it was no use.

"Is the baby thirsty?" he said as he grabbed a handful of snow and began mashing it into my face. Then his friend reached down and grabbed my pants, and tried to undo them. I managed to kick him in the face and he fell back.

"Ow! You little shit."

He hit me in the thigh with his fist and I drew my legs up in pain. Thornton proceeded to slap my face from left to right, each slap growing progressively harder, until finally, he doubled up his fist and hit me in the eye. I thought I was going to pass out. His friend sat on my legs and once again reached for the button at the top of my pants and I forgot about my eye.

And then, I felt Thornton's weight lift from my body, and as I wiped the snow from my face I could see Neely, dressed only in his robe and slippers, holding him by the back of his hair. Thornton grimaced in pain as Neely pushed him aside, then quickly turned and kicked the other boy off of me, who then jumped to his feet.

"Go on, get out of here, both of you, before I give you a good whipping."

I started to get up as both boys, fists clenched, moved toward Neely. I could hear voices in the distance and turned to see two orderlies running toward us. Thornton and his friend saw them, too, and began to move away.

"Dirty Nigger!" yelled Thornton. His friend reached down and quickly formed a snowball and tossed it at Neely, hitting him square in the face. Both boys laughed out loud.

Thornton glared at me. "And I'll be seeing you again," he said.

Neely stood frozen, watching the two boys as they ran off into the trees, his face still covered with snow. There was a look in his eyes, a look new to me, tired, but not like the tired I'd seen after an afternoon of playing catch. They seemed to be set deeper in his skull, not allowing any light to escape, as though he were trying to look inside his own body, which was slowly closing in on itself and beginning to shrink like a snowman on a warm spring afternoon. He wiped the snow from his face and held it momentarily in his hand. It was cold and wouldn't melt. He brought it back up to his face and rubbed it in till finally it dissipated into flakes, falling like lead tears to the ground. I looked at his feet, almost expecting to see a puddle of water. His knees were trembling. Then, very abruptly, they stopped.

"Are you alright?" he said

I looked up and my eyes met his, back now from their muse. Any fear or pain that I might have felt a minute earlier was gone now.

"I'm fine."

The orderlies arrived and helped Neely back into his wheelchair and immediately headed for the hospital.

"We gotta get you out of this weather," one of them said and then turned to me. "You better come in, too, let us take a look at you."

I brushed away the snow and followed them.

"That was a damn fool thing to do, coming out here,"

said one of the orderlies.

Neely remained quiet.

"You were great," I said.

The receptionist met us at the door. It was the same girl I'd seen the day of the fire and I realized I hadn't seen Laurie, since then. One of the orderlies told her to call my house but I told him I could walk home.

"What's your number?" she asked.

"Nobody's home."

Neely winked at me.

"Let's get you back in bed," said the orderly.

"Call the Yellow Cab," said Neely. "Tell them to send his father."

The second orderly took me by the hand. "Come on, we'll get you cleaned up."

"I'm okay, really."

"Come see me tomorrow," Neely said as he was wheeled away. While the girl was busy dialing the cab company, I tiptoed out the front door, grabbed my sled and headed for home. I don't know why, but I did not want my father coming to the hospital to pick me up. I didn't want him involved in my relationship with Neely, whether that was for my protection or my father's, I couldn't say. My body ached all over and my swollen eyelid began to close out the light. I thought about Thornton and his friend; they could be out there somewhere, waiting to get at me again, but I didn't care. The fear I had felt when first accosted by them was now replaced with hatred and rage. It was the first time I ever felt like I wanted to see someone dead.

NINETEEN

The day before Christmas I slept late. When I woke, my left eye was swollen and full of sleep. I rubbed it; it felt tender. Frank was already up and gone. The house was quiet. I looked out my window; the storm had passed, the sky was blue. That is to say, it was as blue as it gets that time of year. There was still a thin, shear layer of clouds, very high in the sky, like the swirl of cigarette smoke but motionless. Still, it made for a rather bright, clean morning, and if you stood with your face to the sun and closed your eyes, you could feel the warmth and the promise of spring.

There were more presents under the tree. In addition to the one from Anna, I now had another of about the same size, marked from Santa Claus—meaning my parents—a habit my mother still clung to even though we had long ago abandoned that legend. I was surprised to see these after the conversation my parents had had. Perhaps my father had gone to Uncle Charlie.

Carol and Richard had bought presents for everyone but I didn't see one for me. I double-checked all the packages but I hadn't made a mistake. It wasn't there. I figured they just hadn't gotten around to wrapping it yet and left it at that.

I could smell the smoke from Anna's cigarette and joined her in the dining room. She was reading the paper.

"Where is everyone?"

"Well, it's about time you got up." She set the paper down and a look of horror came over her face. "Michael, what happened to your eye?"

"What?" What's wrong with it?"

She got up from her seat and raced over to me. "It's all black and blue."

"It is?"

We went into the bathroom and sure enough, there it was—my first shiner, and a beauty at that. My swollen eyelid covered half my eye; it was spongy to the touch and surrounded by shades of purple, blue and black.

"What happened?"

"I don't know. Must have done it on my sled."

I hadn't told anyone but Frank about the fight. I didn't want my father dragging me over to see Thornton's brother like he had done with Frank that time he and Thornton got into it at the church. Frank said my father told Father Steven if he ever laid a hand on one of his kids again he'd come back and beat the hell out of him, right in front of God and everyone. Frank said it was pretty embarrassing because it happened right in front of the church, with lots of other people around. Father Philip finally broke it up and he even had to give Father Steven's sermon for him, he was so shook up by the event.

Now, the funny part is, it was Father Steven—not Frank—who told my father about the trouble. And my dad screamed and yelled at Frank before they went over there, had even had to physically throw him in the back of the car to get him to go. So Frank was really surprised to see him get so mad at Father Steven. He had expected to hear a long apology for his son's behavior, a pleading that Frank be allowed to continue on as an altar boy. The way Frank finally figured it was, yelling at us would be tolerated—God knows, we deserved it—but laying a hand on us was a privilege reserved only for him—and my mother, if she could catch us.

Anna put together an ice pack for my eye and then gave me the good news about Martin. My mother had called from work and told her he had improved substantially in the last two days and it looked like he was going to be all right. Anna had wanted to go over to the hospital to see him but didn't want to leave me home alone, so there she sat patiently reading the paper and smoking cigarettes. Now that I was out of bed, she decided to make the walk. I would have gone with her (I wanted to see Neely) but I had a World Series to play and I had told Neely I had a present for him, and I still hadn't figured out what to give him.

Time was running out.

I felt bad that she had waited around for me but I explained to her that I'd been staying home alone during the day since I was nine years old. She gave me an "oh brother" and a hug, grabbed her coat and was out the door.

I think I had already decided subconsciously that unless game six was a complete runaway by the Dodgers, the Yankees would win it. I suppose we all like a little drama, even children, and few things cam compare to the seventh game of a World Series between the Dodgers and Yankees. And besides, now that L.A. had already won three, I felt compelled to make up for that turn of the head in game two. And so, with a shuffle here and a pinch-hitter there, I was able to help the Yankees along to a four-three victory, Ditmar going the distance against Stan Williams—the only Dodger with a winning record in fifty-eight—who had to come out for a pinch-hitter in the sixth inning. I had Padres or Drysdale to choose from for the last game and although I was partial to Drysdale, I had to go with Padres after his brilliant performance in game three. Whitey Ford would be on the mound for the Yankees. A battle of southpaws. But it would have to wait. The day was half gone and I still had to decide on a present for Neely.

I didn't have any money to buy him anything, and in fact, I wasn't getting presents for anyone else. As children, we never exchanged presents. There just wasn't any money and the issue never really came up. The idea was—as we knew it-when Jesus was born, presents were brought to him and so to celebrate that occasion, people gave presents to one another. Children were only on the receiving end of this proposition—which made it even better. Somewhere along the line, this Santa Claus character came into play, a big, jolly fat man dressed in red who managed to fit down our chimney, and had reindeer that could fly. By the time I was around eight years old, I could no longer manage (geometrically) to squeeze that over-fed fellow down that un-yielding brick enclosure. Other doubts followed.

I rummaged through our room looking for something to give. I thought about making another set of my baseball game but I didn't have duplicates of enough baseball cards. Everything else I had was kid stuff: rubber army men, bottle caps, popsicle sticks (These I used to make rafts which we would float down the street during the rainy season.), flimsy cardboard lids to milk bottles (twenty-five would get you a free popsicle), a bag of buckeyes, a bag of acorns, a small gold horse won at the carnival, and my prize possession: an autographed, official major league baseball (also won at the carnival).

I grabbed the ball from my desk and inspected the signatures: Gil Hodges, Mickey Mantle, Don Drysdale, Charlie Neal, to name a few. And there was Satchel Paige. I had seen the name before, but until I met Neely it had no significance.

I had won the ball when I was nine, throwing baseballs at empty metal cans. I had two dollars to spend at the carnival; it took all but fifty cents of it to win the ball, but it was worth it. It hadn't occurred to me at the time that I could probably have purchased the very same ball at any five and dime store, or that the moment I walked away with it, it would be replaced by another, identical to it. No, I was sure this ball was special, that all those great players had gotten together and signed this one, that it had traveled around with the carnival waiting for that special day, that special person, to come along. I was he. I set it in my glove and lay down on the bed to think it over, and fell asleep.

———

I am standing on the mound, and although I can't see myself, in my mind I am grown up. The stands are full of noisy fans, and standing at the plate is Mickey Mantle, but he looks like Thornton. The bases are loaded. I turn to look at the scoreboard. It reads New York—zero, Brooklyn—one. It's the bottom of the ninth inning. It's the World Series, I say to myself, but then I look at the ball in my glove (the new Wilson) and I can't figure out why they let me use my ball with all the signatures on it. Mantle has just stepped up to the plate but the count is already three and two. I think to myself, if he hits a homerun, I'll just reshuffle the cards. I go into my windup and deliver the pitch and Mantle hits a little dribbler between the mound and third base. I try to run it down but I can hardly move. A runner scores. I reach the ball and try to pick it up. The names are gone from it. I bobble the ball a couple of times then finally manage to pick it up and toss it to the plate, but the throw is late; a second runner scores and we lose the game.

When I reach the dugout, Neely hands me a stack of cards. He is wearing his yellow cap but I am thinking he's the manager of the Dodgers. Other players are in the dugout, but their faces are indistinct. I start flipping the cards over, looking for a strike. In the distance, I can hear Frank calling my name, but I can't see him. His voice grows louder and I quickly flip over more cards. Finally, there is a strike. I look around to see if anyone else has noticed it. Father Steven has my ball with the autographs in his hand, but before he can say anything, I feel a hand on my shoulder.

"Hey, wake up. We gotta get ready."

It was Frank. I sat up in bed, totally confused.

"For what?"

"The party."

I looked out the window; it was dark; I had slept all afternoon. Frank had on his best pants and a white shirt. He grabbed a necktie from his drawer.

"Where is everyone?"

"Downstairs. You better get up."

He tied the tie but the thin part was too long. He quickly undid it and started over.

"Have you looked at your eye?"

"What about it?"

"It's practically swollen shut."

His tone of voice made me feel proud, like we were equals, two buddies who had just returned from a fight together, assessing the damage. I played it down.

"It'll go away."

"This damn thing," he said and pulled the tie from around his neck and tossed it on the bed. "I ain't wearing it."

I got out of bed and quickly changed clothes, leaving my tie in the drawer. My dress shoes were a little scuffed up so I had to give them a quick polishing. I could hear footsteps coming up the stairs and looked up to see Carol.

"Are you guys ready to go?"

"I have to finish polishing my shoes."

"Well, you better hurry up, Dad's ready."

"Tell him to hold his horses," said Frank.

"I'll see you over there," she said and started to leave.

"Where you going?"

"I'm riding with Richard."

She was half way down the stairs when Frank called out to her. "I wanna ride with you guys."

"Can't wait...bye."

TWENTY

We picked up Peter on the way to the party. Pat had been invited too, but it seems he and Laurie had planned a Christmas Party all their own. Laurie had called her mother that morning from Florida. She and Pat were married. Of course, Mrs. Grady would eventually spread the word throughout town that Laurie was pregnant and they had to get married, but most people seemed to adopt a wait-and-see attitude. (As it turned out, she was right.)

I thought Peter's father would take it out on him and not let Peter come to the party but Peter said his father rarely knew where Pat was, anyway, and besides, he was passed out drunk by the time we reached their house.

When Peter answered the door, I hardly recognized him. His hair was parted and slicked back and his face washed so clean you could actually see a little rosy hue on his cheeks instead of the perpetual smudge of soil. He had on the same old brown shoes I had seen a thousand times before, but with a lot of polish and elbow grease, Mrs. McBride had somehow managed to extract a final inkling of a shine from them. His pants had been starched and pressed with a crease down the middle, giving them new life, and his shirt was brand new; it had to be. (Nothing Peter wore more than once could ever be made to look brand new again.)

"What are you staring at?"

"Nothing."

I stepped inside and closed the door. In the corner of the living room stood a small tree with a few lights and three packages below it. The room was clean and tidy but the furniture was in total disrepair: the material on the overstuffed chair was worn through to the stuffing, which had lost its form from years of use; lamp shades, once white, were now yellow and cast a pale, sickly hue against the walls, which had probably not been painted in years and were stained with cigarette smoke; there was a coffee table and two small end tables—all of them chipped and scratched—and in the middle of the room, a large oval rug that had been hung over the line and beaten with a broom once too often.

Mr. McBride was sprawled out, face down on the couch, one hand still clenching an empty beer bottle. If Peter or his mother were embarrassed they certainly didn't show it. They had a worn out room filled with worn out furniture and a worn out man. Everything was in its place.

Peter's mother handed him a jacket and then snapped a red bowtie onto his shirt.

"Aw, do I gotta."

"Yes, you gotta."

Peter just shook his head in defeat. "Boy, Thornton musta really clobbered you!" he said, checking out my shiner.

"Doesn't hurt."

"You boys go on now before you wake up Mr. McBride."

"Yeah, that'll happen," said Peter half under his breath. He kissed his mother goodbye and the two of us ran out to the car.

Mrs. McBride stood silhouetted in the doorway, waving to us as we pulled away. Unprepared and unwilling to comprehend the depth of her loneliness, I bore witness only to her diminished figure and the vanishing light as we turned the corner and she slowly closed the door.

As we drove along, Peter continuously fussed with the red bowtie and kept running his fingers inside his collar trying to loosen it. "Why don't you take it off?" I asked.

"I will, later."

————

Charlie and Phoebie lived on Water Street, named that, I suppose, because it ran adjacent to the river, and, on the rare occasion when the river jumped its banks, ran under it. The street was inhabited entirely by Italians, most of them related to my father. When his father arrived from Italy at the turn of the century, he spent a year in Chicago, then moved south, to our town, where he bought the house my grandmother still lived in. There were other Italians on the street but it was, for the most part, family. As my father's brothers grew up, they each bought houses on the street; in fact, of five brothers, my father was the only one who didn't live there.

Charlie's house was the nicest on the block. He had done well in town, investing in real estate, and had subsequently staked all of his brothers in their ventures; all, that is, except for my father. He had, however, bought the house we lived in and let us live there for free.

They held the party in their basement, a remodeled testament to their abundant wealth. There was no foreboding coal bin here; no musty odor here; no perpetually overborne clothesline here; just thick, white carpet, the finest of furniture and an ever-present smell of money. We left our shoes in the entry as we came in.

There were around fifty people there when we arrived and there would be more still to come, mostly relatives. At one end of the room, tables had been set up for dining. There were a half dozen or so round ones that sat six to eight people each; these were for the adults. They were set with the finest china and silver on a pristine white tablecloth with a clinquant trim. And there were bottles of fine wines, reds and whites.

Off to the side was another table comprised of numerous card tables pushed together. It was covered with white sheets and was adorned with utensils and paper plates for the children.

Most of their furniture had been moved up against one wall and covered with sheets and blankets, leaving a small area in the middle of room for dancing.

At the far end of the room was the bar, surrounded now mostly by men, as the women busily prepared the evening's meal. Somehow, Charlie had managed to get hold of a couple of slot machines, which he set up right next to his bar. My father referred to them as the great equalizers. He must have said that ten times that night, especially when someone he didn't particularly care for would lose. He, however, refused to play them.

"That bastard, Charlie, ain't getting any of my money," he'd say, but in a tone of voice that made most people think he was kidding, and in fact it would usually bring a laugh.

I wanted to play one of the machines but there was a long line, so Peter and I started rummaging through the Christmas presents stacked under their tree, a huge one that almost reached the ceiling and was as big around as it was tall. They had had it sprayed white and decorated with crystal clear bulbs and white lights. A silver star adorned the top.

I found a present with my name on it and gave it a shake.

The contents rattled a little, bringing a smile to my face.

"No clothes in there," I said.

"Are all these people here giving you presents?"

"No. Just my Aunt Phoebie."

As we talked, I kept my eye on the slot machine. When the line finally dwindled down to just a few, I grabbed Peter by the arm.

"Come on. Now's our chance."

I dragged him over to the machine and got in line.

"I don't have any money," Peter said.

"I have two quarters. You can use one. But you gotta pay me back."

It took about ten minutes to get a turn. The guy in front of me, an older cousin, must have spent five dollars before he finally gave up in anger; he hadn't hit once.

"What do you do?" asked Peter.

"Just watch," I said as I reached up to the slot and dropped my quarter in. I rubbed my hands together—I had seen men do this playing dice—grabbed the arm and gave it a good hard tug. Time seemed to stand still as I waited for each column to come to a halt, each cherry falling into place a little slower than the one before it. When the third one hit, there was a momentary silence—even the ice in the grown-up's drinks stopped tinkling—and then it started raining quarters. It sounded like a million dollars. I was seeing baseball gloves and bicycles, shiny cars and fancy clothes.

"I won! I won!"

I started scooping up the quarters (turned out to be five dollars), as the crowd gathered tightly around me, voices exclaiming their excitement.

"He won five dollars!"

"I must have put twenty bucks in that bandit and this kid

takes one shot at it and wins. There's no justice."

From behind the crowd I could hear a familiar voice, high pitched with excitement.

"Take the winner off! Take the winner off!"

I stopped gathering up my winnings for a second and looked around, searching for the body behind the voice. Peter stood next to me, quarter in hand. It was Aunt Phoebie. She was closer now.

"Take the winner off. Put another quarter in."

I looked at Peter, then up at the machine as a hand reached over and stuck in a quarter. It was my Uncle Charlie. The crowd grew quiet again and I stopped collecting my winnings. Off to Charlie's side, I could see my father, his eyes glued in anger on Charlie.

"Charlie. Get away from there," said Phoebie. She had a way of stretching certain words out when she spoke. Charlie would become Charrrrlie, Michael,…Miiichael.

The first jackpot bar came to a stop. Charlie took a puff from his cigar. He had a big smile on his face.

"Cosa c'e'?"

"That was Michael's winner. He gets to take it off."

The second jackpot bar pulled into position. My dad was standing right behind Charlie, now. As the orange came to a stop in the third column, Charlie turned to Phoebie.

"Va bene. He can have a the money." But of course, it didn't pay. I grabbed the rest of my quarters and stepped up to the machine behind Charlie. My father turned from the crowd, mumbling to another of his brothers.

"Come on, Charlie, get out of the way," said Phoebie.

"Hey, I save a the boy a quarter."

Charlie laughed and walked away. Phoebie moved in close. A mousy looking woman with buckteeth and bleached blond hair, she was one of the few people on Water Street that my mother could stand. She was kind and generous and, above all, loyal.

"That Charrrrlie," she said, "he's terrrrible. Now don't go putting all your winnings back in the machine."

"I won't."

I put three dollars in one pocket. This I would not touch. I gave Peter another quarter and then I quickly fed seven into the machine, and then cursed myself for not saving it all. Peter put in his two quarters and lost and I told him he didn't have to pay me back. I began to reconsider using the remaining quarters but a voice called out for dinner and we all took our seats.

———

Presents were distributed after dinner. Charlie and Phoebie bought gifts for all the children and many of the adults. Small groups gathered about, opening theirs, sharing their excitement with one another.

I got a plastic replica of Superman, about a foot long with bright blue tights and red cape. It had a catch on the bottom and a large rubber band attached to a stick with which to propel it.

"Alright! This is neat."

I loaded the rubber band and pulled it taut.

"Not in here," yelled Anna.

"Just testing it," I said.

"It's almost time for Midnight Mass," she said. "Are you kids going?"

"Not me," said Frank.

"Me, either," I said.

"I'm going with Richard," said Carol. "Do you want to

come with us?"

"I think I'm going with Dad," said Anna.

But by now, my father was pretty drunk. He had watched as the different presents were opened, making sly jokes and comments about some. As people began to gather their coats and hats he moved toward the door, stepping up the three steps to the landing.

"Let's go. Can't keep God waiting."

"Dad, why don't you ride with us," said Carol.

"No. No, I got a better idea," he said and then opened the door and stuck his head out.

"Taxi! Taxi!"

He closed the door and stepped back into the room. Most of the adults quieted down and now watched him. I set Superman back in the box and moved closer to my father.

"No taxi tonight. Hey, I got it. Let's get Charlie to drive."

Charlie was sitting at one of the tables, smoking a cigar and laughing with a few of the other men. I'm not sure if it was my father they were laughing at or something else.

"How about it, Charlie. We'll make you an honorary cabby."

Charlie took the cigar out of his mouth and stood up. He had a big smile on his face.

"Sure," he said, "we'll take a the Cadillacs."

He looked down at the table to my Uncle Joe. "You can drive Phoebie's," he said.

"I'm not riding in no damn Cadillac," said my father.

Anna stepped up on the landing and handed my dad his hat.

"Come on, Dad," she said, "let's ride with Carol and Richard."

As people began to exit, the crowd forgot about my father

and went back to whatever they were doing. Peter got himself another piece of pie and I dug into my pocket one more time for another quarter. As I pulled down on the lever, I thought about my father and prayed for a jackpot. No such luck.

TWENTY-ONE

I woke early on Christmas Morning and sat up abruptly in bed. The room was cold. Outside, night made its subtle transition to day, and form slowly returned to the landscape as black turned to grey. Frank was deep asleep. I shook him.

"Frank, get up. It's morning."

He rolled over and mumbled something inaudible.

"It's Christmas. Come on. Let's go downstairs."

"I'm sleeping," he said. "Leave me alone."

"But it's Christmas."

Silence.

"Frank."

"Go. Away."

It was the pause between the two words that convinced me of his sincerity. I got out of bed, put on my robe and made my way into the girls' room, a veritable mine field of blouses, bras, and magazines. It was much bigger than the landing where Frank and I slept. We had pleaded for it for us, but my mother insisted that girls needed more privacy than boys, that it would not be right for us to be parading through their room to get to ours.

I tiptoed to the side of the bed. They were fast asleep, Mary cuddled up to Carol, who took the side of the bed closest to the door. I found it strange that a room so disheveled could smell so clean and fresh. I leaned over Carol and whispered to

Mary. That fresh scent seemed to emanate from her.

"Mary. Mary."

Carol looked up at me. "What do you want?"

"It's Christmas."

"It's too early," she whispered. "Go back to bed."

"It's light out."

She sat up, glanced toward the window then dropped back into bed and pulled up the covers.

"It's still dark. Wait a while," she said.

I paused briefly and considered passing through their room into my parents' (There was no hall upstairs connecting the rooms; they just poured into one another.) but I could hear snoring on the other side of their door and so I let the idea go.

I turned and left the room, closed the girls' door behind me and went downstairs into the living room. Since her arrival, Anna had been sleeping on the couch, but she was not there now. Her blankets were folded neatly and stacked at one end. Light poured in from the dining room. I checked under the Christmas tree and discovered a couple of new packages. I tried reading the name tags but there was not enough light in that corner of the room. I held one close to one of the tree lights and tried again, but was soon startled by the sound of Anna's voice.

"Well, it's about time you got up," she said.

"Everyone else is still in bed," I said.

"Well, then, they're going to miss all the fun, aren't they? In addition to her pajamas, she was wearing a sweater and her long, winter coat.

"Are you going somewhere?"

"No. It's freezing in here."

"There's some new stuff here."

"So I noticed."

"I don't see anything shaped like a baseball glove."

"Come on, I made some hot chocolate. I'll get you some while you go put some coal in the furnace."

"Me?"

"Well, I'm not going down there," she said.

And so I ventured into the cellar alone. It was as dark as night down there, but just knowing it was light outside seemed to make a difference for I did not experience the fear that normally accompanied me, especially in the coal bin. I made three trips, stuffing the furnace with coal, stoking the fire to great heights (anything to get everyone out of bed). Kelly and Sport were cuddled close together on their blanket. I brought them some fresh water and went back upstairs.

Anna was reading her bible when I returned. She marked her spot and set it on the table. The house was full of light now and already growing warmer from the coal. I put some marshmallows into my cup.

"When did you get up?"

"Oh, I've been up a long time. You know, at the convent, I get up before the sun every morning. It's my favorite time of day."

"It's a little spooky."

"Oh, not really. It's just quiet. You're used to a lot going on, so the quiet seems strange..." She reached over and ran her fingers through my hair. "...spooky."

"If it's not spooky, why didn't you go into the cellar?"

"Oh, brother. You're beginning to sound like Frank."

I felt just a tinge of pride. This sarcasm was something new for me.

"I wish those guys would hurry up and get up."

"It was a late night last night, Michael. Everyone's tired."

"But it's Christmas. I want to open my presents."

"I know. They're not going anywhere."

"I wonder if Neely's up yet."

"Neely? Oh, yes, your friend at the hospital. How is he doing?"

"Pretty good, I guess. I have his present. I want to take it to him. You're going with me, aren't you?"

"You bet I am. What did you get him?"

"I'll show you."

I ran upstairs and got the baseball, checked for signs of life—everyone was still asleep—and brought it back down to show Anna. She took the ball in her hand and inspected the signatures.

"This must be a very special ball. Who are all these people?"

I took the ball from her, somewhat shocked at her ignorance. "That's Joe Dimaggio. He was on the Yankees."

Anna's face went blank.

"Don't you know who Joe Dimaggio is?"

"No, I'm afraid not. But how did you get all those autographs?"

"Well, I didn't actually get them. I won this at the carnival last year. But it's one of a kind; and they're real signatures. I just hope Neely likes it."

"I'm sure he'll love it. Can I see it again?"

I handed her the ball. As we spoke I occasionally turned my head toward the living room in anticipation. The waiting was driving me crazy.

"Official Major League Baseball," she said. "Who is this guy here...what does it say, Baby Ruth?"

"Babe, Anna. You're thinking of the candy bar."

An hour went by and still no one came down the stairs. I decided to get dressed and go outside; I took the plastic Superman with me. It actually performed quite well. From the back yard I could make it soar all the way over our house to the street out front. There I would shoot it toward Wilson Street, a good fifty yards away—it made it all the way in one flight—turn right at the corner and fly it down Wilson to the alley that ran behind our house, then a final flight down the alley to our back yard. After a few trips around the block I started aiming it at different things: a bird sitting low in a tree—I missed; telephone wires—not a good idea; when it hit the wires it went into a nose-dive, smacking down hard into the street; and even the snowman I had built—I stuck it shoulder deep into its icy stomach.

And so on I went for a good hour or so until finally I heard the screen door slam, and I ran around to the rear of the house. Frank and Mary had come out.

"Is everyone up?"

"Dad's still sleeping," said Mary.

"Let me try that thing," said Frank.

"Don't break it."

"I'm not gonna hurt it," said Frank and I handed him the toy.

He pointed it straight up and pulled the rubber band back further than I had ever attempted. I flinched, fearing it would snap.

"You're gonna snap the rubber band..."

He released the plastic Superman and up he went. The three of us cranked our necks to watch as he soared above the oak tree toward the clouds. The red and blue of his uniform began to lose their definition as he climbed further and further above the earth, and for a moment I thought he wasn't coming back. Then, just as quickly, the color returned and the tiny replica grew larger and larger as it dived toward the ground, a silent streak of blue and red, and it was headed right toward us.

"Look out!" Frank yelled and we all scattered. A second later it crashed, head first, in the very spot where we had stood.

"You broke it!" I said, and reached down to pick it up. There was a small chip out of his head, but other than that, no damage had been done.

"Is it ruined?" asked Mary.

"No, it's okay."

"Told you," said Frank.

"You're not supposed to fly it straight up, Frank."

"Where does it say that?"

"I thought it was going to smash in a million pieces," said Mary.

"Superman can't smash," said Frank. "He's invincible."

I studied Frank's face closely as he spoke, searching for that hint of irony, but I couldn't tell if he was serious or not.

"Except for kryptonite," I added.

"My turn," said Mary.

"Let's go inside and open our presents," I said.

"Let me fly it once, first."

"Let her try it," said Frank. "She can't hurt it."

I showed Mary how to load the rubber band. She pulled it back as far as she could but was having difficulty steadying it.

"It's gonna hit the house," I said and Frank put his hand on hers and helped pull the toy back a little and directed it above the house.

"Got it?"

"Okay," she said and Frank let go. Mary stood frozen,

unable to let go, Superman weaving and shaking in her hands.

"Let loose," said Frank.

"Let it go!" I shouted.

She finally released. It headed straight for the roof. I held my breath as it barely cleared the top of the house and continued on toward the front yard. We ran after it.

As we got to the front of the house, Superman was nowhere to be seen. A coal truck had passed by and was almost to the corner.

"It must be on the roof," I said.

"It cleared the roof," said Frank.

"Maybe it's across the street."

"Wouldn't have gone that far."

The truck stopped at the corner then made a right turn and continued on.

"Maybe it landed in the truck," said Mary.

Frank and I looked toward the truck, then to the backyard. We both drew imaginary arcs over the house with our heads. Both ended in the street. We took off yelling after the truck, Mary close behind, but it was no use. We went a couple of blocks and then gave up as the truck disappeared in the distance. The three of us walked quietly back home. Maybe somewhere that night, Superman would show up in somebody's coal bin. Maybe even mine.

"I'm sorry," said Mary as we reached the porch.

"It doesn't matter," I said.

"Maybe he didn't land in the truck," said Frank. "Maybe he just flew away. Back to Krypton."

"Or the Fortress of Solitude," I said quietly. "He could have gone there."

TWENTY-TWO

We came in quietly through the porch door. Everyone was up now and having coffee in the dining room.

"You guys are awfully quiet," said my mother. She seemed to be in good spirits.

"We lost Superman," said Mary.

"Superman? Oh, your toy."

"It's okay," I said.

"Maybe he flew away," said my father, who then chuckled quietly.

"Sam." said my mother.

"Well, he is Superman, isn't he?" He laughed again. "We'll get you another one," he added, as if that's how things were always done around our house. Something gets lost or destroyed and we just go out and replace it.

"Guess who's coming home today," said Anna.

"Martin!" said Mary. "Is he better?"

"The doctor says he's well enough to come home. We're going to go pick him up this afternoon. You kids wanna go?"

"I do. I wanna see Neely. Can we open our presents now?"

"Richard's not here yet," said Carol. "He's bringing a few things."

"Come on, we've been waiting all morning."

"Let's go," said my mother. "Richard won't mind."

My mother passed out the presents to everyone. I had three packages: one from Anna and two from my parents. Frank and Mary had the same (my parents always tried to keep things equal). There was one each for Anna and Carol. Anna handed my parents their presents from her, and my father gave my mother hers. As I suspected, Anna got me pajamas. There was a cowboy shirt from my parents–it was light blue with dark blue cuffs and collar–and in their other package, some hard-rubber army men. I already had some of these but the dog had chewed many of them up; others were partially melted and twisted out of shape from battle. (I tried my best for realism. A trail of lighter fluid leading up to a pile of caps made quite a little explosion.)

Frank got clothes—pajamas from Anna (who would have guessed?), a shirt and a new pair of jeans from my parents, and from Carol and Richard, a pocketknife complete with bottle opener and corkscrew. My mother, who was growing tired of having her paring knives disappear, had undoubtedly suggested this.

As everyone finished opening their presents, I looked discreetly around the room, hoping against hope to find another package for me. There were none. It had all come and gone so fast after weeks of anticipation. It was like lighting a fuse to an explosive that never goes off. I was happy to get the shirt. I needed new army men. Pajamas? Things were out of synch. In my baseball game, things happened. I made them happen. I would not have the seventh game of the World Series called in the ninth inning because of rain. I would not let Duke Snider sit out the season because of a turn of a card. Who was turning my cards?

I looked over to see my father open a present. It was a plain brown cowhide wallet. He opened it up and looked inside. Not that he was checking for money, but rather as a courtesy to Anna, who had given it to him. (It was, of course, empty.)

"Thanks," he said, "this is just what I needed."

Then, my mother got up and went into the other room. Mary was trying to stand her new doll up, but it kept falling down on its face. (They always seem to make the feet way too small on dolls, as if they believed the damn things could somehow balance themselves.) Carol was admiring the scarf Anna had gotten my mother and Frank had already cut a branch from the Christmas tree with his new knife and begun whittling away, a small pile of shavings gathering at his feet. I could tell it was bothering my father, but he managed to stifle himself. My mother returned with a box. It was not wrapped. She handed it to my father.

"I didn't have time to wrap this," she said.

My father opened it up and removed from it an old, yet beautiful, violin.

"I had it restrung," she said.

There was a moment of complete silence, shortly broken by Anna.

"Play something, Dad."

I had seen it before, years ago, but had forgotten all about it. I was six, maybe seven at the time, and had been looking for something in my parents' closet. I had to stand on a chair to reach the highest shelf and there it was, covered with dust, a couple of strings missing. I took it down and plucked at it a few times, then quickly returned it to the shelf and went back to looking for whatever it was I was after. It had never occurred to me that my father played it. After all, it was in pretty bad shape. Who would ever let their instrument deteriorate like that? I never gave it another thought.

"It's been awhile," said my father. He had already begun tuning it, almost, it seemed, subconsciously. My mother reached under the couch and pulled out the bow.

"I almost forgot," she said as she handed it to him.

We waited patiently as he finished tuning. Frank even stopped his whittling. My father looked at me.

"Here's one you should know."

He placed the instrument on his shoulder, then he gently dropped his chin onto the body to hold it in place. He slowly ran the bow across the strings a couple of times, occasionally bouncing it lightly off of them. All this, I assumed, was part of some well-worn ritual. The song began and I recognized it right away—The Tennessee Waltz. He got a couple of measures into the melody and then missed a note. He started over. I watched his fingers closely. They were long and slender. I had never noticed that before. As he hit each note, his hand would vibrate, but ever so slightly, giving the note a rich, sweet sound. He kept his eyelids closed throughout but I could see his eyes moving behind them as if they were striking the notes. As he went into the bridge he missed another note. He stopped abruptly and set the violin down.

"Don't stop," said Carol.

"Play some more, Sam," said my mother.

"I'm out of practice," he said and then got up from the couch. "We should probably get over to the hospital."

His eyes darted about the room, landing nowhere for more than a split second. Then he turned to Frank.

"Clean up that mess before we go," he said and walked out of the room.

"What's buggin' him?" said Frank.

"Don't worry about it," said my mother. "You kids get your jackets. We'll clean this up when we get back. Frank, just put those cuttings in the trash, OK?"

"I'm going to wait here for Richard," said Carol.

"We won't be gone long."

Frank reached down and grabbed a handful of twigs from the branch he had hacked up. It seemed absurd, considering the floor was covered with pine needles. We left our packages there on the floor and went for our coats.

Up in our room I could hear the car start and then, shortly after, a couple of light beeps on the horn. I grabbed Neely's present. Frank was sitting on the bed.

"You better hurry up."

"I'm staying here," said Frank.

"Don't you wanna meet Neely?"

"Not today."

The horn beeped again, louder this time and longer.

"You better get going before he has a cow," said Frank.

———

It was a short but deadly quiet ride to the hospital. My father seemed very far away. Every once in a while my mother would look over at him and I could see her lips start to move as if she were about to speak, but then she would just look away in silence.

I was more than happy to see our journey come to an end. Anna went with my parents up to the second floor to get Martin. Mary went with me. We waited for the girl at the desk to turn her back and then we quickly sneaked by her. In my visits to Neely I had come to recognize some of the patients on his floor and had even stopped to say hello to them on occasion, my fear and repulsion for them having gradually dissipated. I waved to a few of them now as we passed through the corridor.

"It stinks in here," said Mary.

I motioned for her to be quiet. "I know," I whispered. "Sometimes they can't hold it long enough to get to the bathroom."

"Oh. You mean, they just go in their beds?"

"Yeah. One thing's for sure, I'm never going to a hospital if I get sick."

"Well, where would you go?" She sounded genuinely concerned for my health.

"I don't know. I'd just stay home."

"What if you got really sick?"

"I won't."

The door to Neely's room was shut. I knocked lightly and when there came no answer, grabbed the knob.

"Maybe he's sleeping," said Mary.

"I gotta give him his present. I'll just leave it on the bed."

We tiptoed into the room. The curtain between the two beds was pulled all the way back to the wall. Both beds were empty and made up. I felt just a tinge of panic in my stomach.

"There's nobody here," said Mary.

I walked over to Neely's bed. The bottle of fluid and connecting tube were gone. The magazine I had seen on the table during my previous visit had also vanished. I ran to the door and checked the number. We were in the right room. Mary opened the closet door.

"There's some clothes in here," she said.

There was a black suit, a couple of shirts covered in clear plastic, two pair of shoes and a small duffel bag. I opened the bag. Inside there were socks and t-shirts, some pencils, a packet of chewing tobacco and a scrapbook. I opened the book. It was filled with pictures, mostly of ballplayers, one of Neely with his arm around an attractive woman. He couldn't have been more than thirty in the picture, but I recognized him right away. He was thin and muscular, no signs of gray in his dark, curly hair. I flipped through the pages, then closed the book and zipped up the bag. I started to close the closet door, and then I saw it, high on a shelf, the tip of its yellow beak extending slightly over the edge. Neely's hat.

I ran toward the door.

"Where are you going?" Mary hollered after me but I did not slow down to answer her. I ran into a nurse just outside the door and she dropped a tray. The sound of shattering glass silenced her complaint. I just kept moving.

Both elevators were occupied so I took the stairs down to the basement, Mary close behind. I burst through the morgue doors and flipped on the light. There was a body on one of the tables, covered with a sheet. I approached it slowly, fearfully, yet still clinging to a thin thread of hope. Mary was out of breath.

"What are you doing? I don't like it in here."

I grabbed hold of a corner of the sheet, held it in my hand for what seemed like hours and then slowly pulled it back to Neely's shoulders. Mary jumped back.

It was as though someone had pulled a curtain around us. I could hear the sound of Mary's voice in the distance but I have no idea what she was saying. I reached out and touched Neely's blotchy skin. It was cool and dry. His eyelids were closed and the thought crossed my mind that if I could only open them the life would return to him. They were shut tight, yet there were no signs of strain in his face. Life was shut out. Tiny droplets of water began to run down his cheeks and at first I thought he was crying but quickly realized they were my own tears. I embraced him, half-expecting a miracle, yet fully aware of his absence.

I don't know how long I stayed in that position, my head buried in his chest, my arms gathering him in, trying to hold him together, like so many fallen leaves. Eventually, sounds began to penetrate the curtain, and then the warmth of a hand on the back of my neck.

"Michael. Michael, come on, get up."

It was Anna. Her voice was soft, almost lyrical. She gently pried me away from him. I noticed for the first time that I still held the ball, gripped like Neely had shown me—in another life?—for a fastball. I set it down next to his lifeless body. Mary stood by Anna's side expelling a shower of tears, and I wondered why she was crying.

———

Richard and Carol were excited to see Martin upon our return. I bolted past them and up the stairs, and dived into bed next to Frank, spilling his milk in his lap.

"Hey, watch it!"

My head hung over the bed, and on the floor, directly below me, was my game. I reached down and flung the pile of cards across the room.

"What's the matter with you?"

"Nothing," I said, or cried. "Leave me alone."

"You spilled my milk all over the place."

I could feel him get up from the bed. I grabbed my pillow and buried my head, saying nothing; shortly thereafter I heard his footsteps trail away down the stairs. I lay there for a while, weeping, too many thoughts in my head. Soon after Frank's departure, more footsteps entered the room and then my mother's voice.

"Michael, why don't you get up and come downstairs. Richard and Carol have something for you."

I kept quiet.

"Don't you want to talk about it?"

I reached up and placed my hands on the pillow, holding it tight to my head. I could feel my mother grab the pillow and try to pull it away but I quickly tightened my grip.

"Come on," she said, and pulled harder. I resisted. Her voice raised in pitch. "Michael. Let go."

She pulled the pillow away from me and I quickly sat up, tears gushing down my face.

"He's dead! It's not fair! It's not fair!" I tried to grab the pillow from her but instead she pulled me close to her.

"I'm sorry," she said, and now she was crying, too.

Someone came to the top of the stairs—I don't know who, maybe Mary (the step was light)—but my mother quickly sent whomever it was away. It felt good to be held, and I fell asleep in her arms.

When I awoke, it was dark and my first thoughts were of that first afternoon in the morgue, hiding in the vault. The feelings of anxiety lessened as my eyes adjusted to the room and I recognized the familiar surroundings. Voices drifted in from downstairs. I sat up in bed. I felt exhausted and very sad, but the tears had stopped. I got out of bed and walk slowly down the steps.

Everyone was there. The rocking chair creaked beneath the weight of my mother as she gently rocked Martin, fast asleep in her lap. My father interrupted his conversation with Anna to pour himself a shot of bourbon. As my presence became known, a quiet settled over the room. Their eyes were on me and it was unsettling.

Anna got up from her chair. "You must be hungry," she said, breaking the uneasy silence, and slowly people returned to their business. "Come on. I'll make you a sandwich."

"I don't want anything right now," I said.

"Are you sure?"

"I'm not hungry."

Carol reached down beside her chair and grabbed a box. She brought it to me.

"This is from Richard and me. Do you want to open it now, or would you rather wait?"

I took the box from her. It was square, big enough to hold a basketball, but not that heavy.

"Come in and sit down," my mother said, quietly, so as not to disturb Martin.

I sat on the edge of the couch, tearing at the ribbon, managing only to turn the bow into a knot. Frank reached over with his knife and cut it. I tore away the paper and pulled off the lid. Inside, under a white sheet of tissue paper was the glove.

How can I explain the feelings that rushed through me, colliding with one another like two opposing trains on the same track. I had wanted that mitt more than anything, and there it was. I should have been thrilled. Had it arrived that morning, I could have greeted it with all the proper emotions but now it only served to remind me of Neely. I recalled that first day when I showed up at the hospital with my old glove, the look of shock on Neely's face and then just as quickly his acceptance of the situation. We would work with what we had.

It seemed a cruel hoax that God should try to buy me off in this way. And yet, I could not deny the seduction. The smell of the soft leather overwhelmed me. I wanted to reach in and try it on. I wanted to oil the pocket with saddle soap and wrap a ball up in it with twine. I wanted to be happy and yet I felt I had no right to be. It didn't seem fair to Neely.

I could feel the tears welling up inside, and I pushed them down. At that moment the most important thing in the world to me was that I would not cry, that I would not be weak, that I would not indulge in any self-pity. I looked across the room to my father, slowly sipping his drink. I glanced over at Frank. I was not as strong as Frank, but I was not my father, either. Neely had told me as much, and now I understood. I could see the space that separates each of us from one another, the form and content that defines who we are and where we leave off.

Frank nudged me in the shoulder with his fist. "Let's see it," he said.

I reached into the box, retrieved the glove and stuck it on my left hand. It seemed to fit me better than when I had tried it on that day in the store. I half-heartedly pounded my fist into the pocket, and then a second time with more force.

"Thanks," I said to Carol and then looked to Richard. "It's great."

TWENTY-THREE

A couple of days after Neely's death, a woman came to our house. I was in my room gathering up the cards I had scattered about the room, when I heard the car pull up in front. It was a yellow cab like my father drove but I knew right away it wasn't him. He always parked in the driveway. I watched as she exited the taxi and ambled up the snow-covered walkway to the front porch, her short stocky frame leaning tentatively upon a wooden walking stick. Nestled in her other arm was a paper bag, the size of a grocery bag. The taxi sat idling at the curb as she drew nearer to the front door. I knew from the color of her skin that she was there to see me. I let go of the curtain and rushed down the stairs to greet her. She was slightly out of breath when I opened the door.

"You Michael?"

"Yes, ma'am."

She peered over the top of her glasses, her chocolate eyes swimming in a face much younger than her twisted body would suggest. A large swath of gray meandered through her wavy black hair then disappeared beneath her scarf.

"Yes, I suppose you are. You are a little one, at that."

I shrugged my shoulders.

"Do you wanna come in?"

"No, boy. I'm just makin' a delivery. Cornelius wanted

you to have these things." She nodded toward the bag and I took it from her and set it inside.

"Are you his wife?"

She laughed. "Oh, child, no. No, Cornelius only had one love: that was baseball. I'm his sister."

I looked down at the bag. "Well, maybe you should keep this stuff."

"No, that's all for you. I got mine, already, what there was to get. Cornelius was a simple man. Now, how 'bout helpin' an old lady down these steps. I'm afraid if I fall down I won't be able to get back up."

I took her arm and helped her down the two steps. We started toward the taxi. She moved very slowly.

"Cornelius and me growed up right here in this very town. Course, Cornelius left a long time ago. He weren't one to stay put. I s'pose he will now, rest his soul."

"He never told me he had a sister."

"Well, Cornelius never liked talkin' much about himself."

We reached the taxi and I helped her inside.

"Oh, I almost forgot. He said to tell you not to forget to follow through in your delivery. Said you'd know what he meant."

"Did he say anything else?"

"No, boy, that was it. I didn't have much time with him. I will tell you this. Your time together meant a lot to him. He never had no children of his own"

She pulled the door shut and rolled down the window.

"Can I visit him?"

"Lord, child, ain't nothin' to visit. I'm takin' his ashes up to Chicago to the baseball field there."

"Wrigley Field?"

"That where the Cubs play?"

"Yes, ma'am."

"Well, that's where I'm lettin' 'em go."

She took a hanky from her purse and wiped her eyes. "Crazy ol' fool, wasted his life playin' a damn fool game. Don't you go doin' that, boy. You end up jus' like Cornelius."

She rolled up her window and the cab drove away. I stood and watched her until they disappeared, then turned toward the house. I could see Mrs. Grady peeking through her curtain. When she saw me look at her she let it fall shut.

I took the bag up to my room and emptied it out on the bed. There was the scrapbook I had seen in his room, a baseball shirt with number seventeen sewn on to the back, the yellow hat, and the shoe-box filled with little memorabilia.

I opened the scrapbook. I recognized the first few pictures from before. The one with him and the young woman was gone. I assumed it was he and his sister. I turned through the pages. There was another picture, very faded, of a young boy, about my age, standing in a crouched position, baseball bat over his shoulders as if he were about to take a swing. The boy had a very serious look on his face as if that swing were about to determine the outcome of the most important event. I took the picture out of the plastic and set it on the bed.

There were dozens of pictures, some of whole teams, others with two or three players, their arms wrapped around one another, their youth and vitality still evident in the faded snapshots. I turned to the last page and a piece of paper fell out from behind one of the pictures. It was a letter. I read it.

Cornelius,

I'm writing to let you know that I have met someone and that I am engaged to be married. He is a good man, a teacher, and he wants the same things that I want: a home and family. I waited two years but it is apparent to me now that I was wrong to ask you to change your life for me. You love baseball. It's your dream and I hope you get everything from it that you want. Dear Cornelius, please don't hate me for this, and please don't try and change my mind, as it has been made up. I hope this letter finds you in good health.

Sincerely, Janelle

———

It took me a moment to make sense of what was before me, but then I recalled the story Neely had told me about his "friend." I folded up the letter and tucked it away beneath the picture. I thought of Neely's sister, that she should have the letter, but I had no idea how to reach her. Then I gathered up the rest of the things and replaced them in the bag— except for the one picture and the hat. I placed the hat on top of my head. It fell down to my ears but I didn't care. I was determined to grow into it.

I put the bag in the closet and returned to my bed. The Dodger and Yankee baseball cards were mixed together in a pile and I began separating them. There was still one game left to play in the series but I felt uninspired. I looked down at the cards. Neely's picture should have been on one of those. His name should have been on the lips of every young boy who ever picked up a baseball. I reached over to the picture of the young boy and set it atop one of the baseball cards.

Of course, that was it. There would be a seventh game, after all. But there would be a new pitcher on the mound for the Dodgers.

I made a couple of other changes in the line-up for that

final game. I switched Hodges to clean-up and moved Snider up one notch against the left-handed Ford. I put Roseboro behind the plate (after all, he was the Dodger catcher at this point), and Zimmer at short.

The first nine cards I turned up were strikes—that had never happened before—putting a quick end to the top of the first. The Dodgers took the field and I handed Neely the ball and ran back to the dugout. The crowd fell silent as the young right-hander went to work. The first inning was a little shaky (That was to be expected. After all, Neely had never faced any of these batters before today.), the Yankees scrambling for a run on a single and stolen base by Kubek, a sacrifice fly by Skowron and a single by Mantle.

Hodges led off the second inning with a double, got as far as third on a ground out to the right side, but died right there as Cimoli struck out and Roseboro popped to short. The Yankees went down in order in the second inning, Neely picking up two strike-outs, his first in the majors. It looked like I might have a pitcher's duel on my hands.

The third inning went quietly, one hit for the Dodgers and none for the Yankees, but in the fourth, things started moving. Snider led off with a single and Hodges doubled. Stengel walked out to the mound to talk to Ford and it was decided they would walk Furillo and pitch to Cimoli, figuring they'd give up a run for a double play. (For an intentional walk, I'd simply turn over the next four cards, treating each of them as a ball. As it turned out, one of those four was a single, and I was feeling a little upset about that, but I had made up my mind: this time there would be no second chances.)

The first pitch to Cimoli was a strike. I moved the three runners away from the bags, giving them all a pretty good lead. The infield was back for the double play. I took a breath and turned over the next card: long fly ball. I quickly shuffled the sub-pile and turned over the top card: Ball is caught, runners advance one base. I was tempted to try and stretch it for another base, but Hodges was not a great runner so I settled for one. Johnny Roseboro stepped in for his first at bat in the series and was promptly walked (intentionally). Once again the bases were loaded but this time Stengel got what he wanted: Zimmer hit the first pitch on a line to Bill Skowron. With Rosoboro taking his lead at first, all Skowron had to do was step on the bag for a quick double play.

The Yankees went quietly in the fifth but in the bottom of the sixth, Neely started to fall apart. He walked the first two batters, got Kubek on a pop up, but then McDougald singled, scoring one run and leaving runners on the corners. I picked up Neely's picture.

"How are you feeling, Neely?"

"I gotta tell you, boy, I'm a little tired. Can't seem to keep the ball down."

"I don't wanna take you out."

"If it was anybody else, what would you do?"

"But I wanted you to pitch the whole game."

"I'm all done, son. Take me out now and finish your game."

I set Neely's picture in the dugout area and brought in Klippstein to face Bauer and Mantle. Klippstein would be due up second in the seventh, so I figured I'd bat for him and bring in Drysdale for the last three innings. Klippstein walked Bauer on four pitches and Mantle promptly tripled to right field and all three runners scored. At the end of six it was five-one, New York. I looked over at the picture of Neely. Did he wink?

Meanwhile, Whitey Ford was sailing along, retiring the

side in order in the seventh. Since the short-lived rally in the fourth, the Dodgers had managed only one base hit, a single by Gilliam in the fifth. Things looked bad.

We got two quick runs in the eighth on a couple of singles and a double, but Duren came in and quickly put out the fire, striking out Cimoli and Roseboro. We were down to our last three outs.

Zimmer led off the ninth with a single. Gray hit for Drysdale and flew out, advancing Zimmer to second and removing any chance for a double play. Gilliam singled, sending Zimmer to third, but Neal struck out, so that when Duke Snider stepped up to the plate, we were two runs behind with one out to go.

I got up off the floor. My legs were stiff from sitting and the room had gotten stuffy. I opened up the window. The cool air felt good on my face. I watched a couple of squirrels chase each other around a tree for a few minutes, then returned to the game.

I placed my hand on the stack of cards, took a deep breath and flipped one over. Ball one. A sigh of relief. Ball two. I placed the Gil Hodges card in the on-deck spot, visions of a grand slam filling my head. Strike! As I fingered the next card I saw the word (double) in my mind and when I flipped it over, there it was. Zimmer scored and Gilliam advanced to third, but I was not about to settle for that. I decided to send him to the plate. It seemed a foolish thing to do with Hodges due up—if I would have stopped and thought about it I probably wouldn't have sent him (play for a tie at home; play to win on the road)—but I seemed to be working on automatic at this point. I grabbed the stolen base pile—my heart was pounding—gave it a quick shuffle, grabbed the top card and held it up in front of me for a few seconds, then flipped it over.

206

I stared at that card for a full two minutes, waiting, I suppose, for the emotion to hit. But for some reason, I didn't feel that bad. The season was over and I had lost the World Series. All those games, all that planning had ended in defeat, yet I didn't feel like a loser. In that instant when Gilliam's card was approaching home and my hand was on the pile of stolen base cards, I felt, for the first time in my life, like I really understood the game.

I gathered up all my baseball cards and the three-by-fives, wrapped them with rubber bands, put them back in the shoebox (along with the picture of Neely) and set it in my drawer. (I never bothered looking at the next few cards in the pile. I guess I didn't want to test myself that far.) Maybe next year.

TWENTY-FOUR

I stayed away from Clark Street for the rest of the winter, spending most of my time after school in the back yard, practicing. I had to replace the head on my snowman a couple of times due to wild pitches, and of course Peter seemed to derive great pleasure from destroying one whenever possible. By early spring, it had begun to melt, and as it shrunk I began to see myself as growing larger. I also felt I was developing into a pretty damn good pitcher.

My father left for California the second week in March. Anna was returning to the convent and would be taking the train with him as far as St. Louis.

My mother made us all get dressed up in our best clothes and lined us up in the living room to say good-bye. My father went down the line, kissing us each on the forehead, telling us to mind our mother. When he got to Frank, he shook his hand and told him he was the man of the house while he (my father) was gone. This gesture of trust toward Frank confused me. Weren't they enemies? Was this my father's way of making peace, of saying he was sorry? He had lost the battle with my mother and was now heading to the west coast to find a job and make a new life for us. In his defeat had he come to realize what he had been doing to Frank?

We walked them outside. Most of the snow was gone now. Patches of dandelions had already begun to sprout. My father kissed my mother on the lips—I had never seen this happen before—and got into my uncle Charlie's Cadillac. I prayed he wouldn't find a job, that he'd be back soon to tell us we weren't leaving. Anna took me aside. I hated to see her go.

"I thought you weren't going back."

"It's where I belong, Michael."

"But you could stay here."

"No, I can't. Someday, and not too long from now, you'll have to make your move too. That's the way it works. You'll understand when the time comes."

"I don't wanna understand," I said, but I already did. Life was an ugly but democratic process of saying goodbye.

She smiled and gave me a hug. "I have to go. I'll write you."

She hugged everyone good-bye then got into the back seat of the Cadillac and they drove away.

———

A week before Little League tryouts, I unwrapped my glove and got Frank to spend a whole day catching for me. The transition to a real baseball was easy. It was solid and perfectly round and did not—unlike the snowballs—feel as though it were about to crumble in my hand. I was convinced I would be pitching in the Majors, hopefully with the V.F.W., for they always had the best team in town. I also liked the color of their uniforms, green letters and and green hat.

Tryouts were held at the Little League field behind the armory. The field backed up to the bluff twenty feet above the Vermilion River. Homeruns hit early in the season were lost to the swift currents, but as summer progressed and the river narrowed, balls could be retrieved along the bank. Of course, many of them would disappear anyway, as spectators would swoop down to the water's edge and snatch them up. Eventually, the concessionaires started offering free sodas for any ball returned; it helped a little.

I had secured many a free drink myself, but this year would be different. This year I would be on the field; I was sure of it.

I made the walk that Saturday in May by myself. It was a beautiful day, sunny and warm with a light breeze teasing the new foliage overhead. The closer I got to the armory, the more boys I saw, many with brand new gloves, some carrying their rubber cleats over their shoulder (I hadn't gotten mine yet.), tied together by the laces.

I reached the field and there must have been two hundred boys there, eager for action. Many I knew from school, the rest were either from St. Anthony or St. Francis. And there were older boys, too, who had come to watch the younger ones tryout. They strutted about with their uniform shirts, making it clear for all to see, they had already been placed on their teams.

I joined up with a couple of boys I knew and began playing catch. I could feel my stomach growling and I fought to hold the anxiety away, but when the man blew the whistle and called out for all of us to get into groups according to our position, I grew weak and felt as if I were going to throw up.

I got into line behind the other potential pitchers. There were about twenty of us, and I was the shortest. We stood patiently waiting as the man dispersed the outfielders to the field—this was the largest group—a good thirty-five to forty boys. Each boy was handed a placard with a number on it and an attached string to hang around the neck, and that number was then jotted down on a piece of paper next to the boy's name. The same was done for infielders. Two third basemen, two second, two shortstops and two first basemen sent out at a time.

Once these groups were put in place, another man started hitting balls to them, calling out their number before each swing of the bat, an assistant jotting down the results of each attempted catch.

Pitchers and catchers were taken off to the side of the field. There were only four catchers (eventually, boys from other positions would be turned into catchers—reluctantly) so each pitcher would have to wait in line for a chance to pitch. We divided up and scrambled for position but before I could secure a spot, the man pulled me off to the side.

"You sure you're a pitcher?" he asked.

"Yes, sir."

He took a deep breath, then looked out into the over-crowded out field.

"This your first year?"

"Uh-huh."

"Well, I'll tell you what, son. There are a lot of boys here wanna be pitchers and most of them are a lot bigger than you, and some of them have already played in the majors. You'd have a much better chance in the outfield."

"But I wanna be a pitcher."

"Well, have it your own way. Go ahead and get back in line."

I was last in line and had to wait close to an hour for my turn to pitch. Some of the boys ahead of me were good. Most were pretty wild, but they were strong, and I could see that with a little practice they might learn to control their pitches and at least have a chance. At that age, a batter is easily intim-idated by speed.

Each boy was given fifteen pitches, but by the time I arrived to throw, it was obvious the man had already made most of his choices. A few of the boys were stopped after five or six pitches, others were asked to throw more.

I grabbed the ball for my first pitch and, without thinking, went into my windup and delivered. The ball went two feet wide of the catcher and bounced across the grass. A few boys laughed. Another ball was handed to me. The man judging us had his head buried in papers. I took a deep breath and went through my routine: check the grip; see the spot; one-thirty; whip the ball; follow through. I went into my wind-up and delivered a perfect strike. I could tell by the echo as the ball hit the mitt, I had stung the boy's hand. The man looked up from his papers as the ball was tossed back to me.

Again I went through the routine and again I threw a perfect strike. A few complimentary murmurs buzzed the air and the man set his pencil down and watched as I took the ball again and delivered my third strike in a row. Then, just as I was about to toss again, another man came up to the one watching me. They exchanged a few words. I went into my wind-up and half way through my delivery the first man (the one keeping score) called out.

"Okay, fellows. That's it for now. We'll be contacting you in a few days to let you know how you did. Now remember, if you don't get chosen for the Majors, you can still play in the Minors, so don't be discouraged."

I went up to the man.

"Excuse me, sir. I didn't get to throw very many..."

He looked at his notebook. "Number eighteen. I got you down here."

"But I only got to throw four pitches."

"Son, there are a lot of boys here. Now, I saw you pitch

and I got it down, right here. Just be patient."

He patted me on the head and walked away.

———

It was a miserable weekend. I stayed close to the phone, half afraid they would call and half afraid they wouldn't. Finally, on Sunday night, my mother answered the phone, one step ahead of me. She handed it to me.

"Yes, sir. Yes, sir, I know. But I only...I understand. Sure, I will. Next Saturday."

I didn't make it. I'd done well, he said, but not quite well enough. I felt cheated. All those snowballs I'd made, hours spent out in the cold. I'd been given four pitches to prove myself and I'd done well. Why had I been treated so unfairly? I made up my mind I would not play in the minors—they weren't even given uniforms, just t-shirts with different colored sleeves—but when Saturday rolled around, I grabbed my glove and headed for town.

There were no tryouts involved. Everyone who wanted to play was guaranteed a place on a team. In fact, the teams had already been picked when I got there. I was handed a white t-shirt with blue sleeves—we would be the Dodgers—given a practice schedule and a position. I would be pitching. We spent a couple of hours working out together that day, a hodge-podge collection of boys: the overweight, the near blind, the uncoordinated. Many had never touched a baseball before and when I warmed up with a catcher, a few gathered around to watch. It seemed I had found my place.

For two weeks I went to practice regularly. Our coach was a high school boy who did his best to try and whip us into shape. At our third practice, he had us play a game of over-the-line. I pitched to nine batters and only one of them hit the ball, a little pop-up to second base (the fielder dropped it). I suppose I should have felt good that I had done so well, that all that practicing had paid off, but I didn't. Most of these boys had never swung a bat before. I might as well have expected my snowman to get a base hit.

Two phone calls changed everything. The first was received by way of a message one day after school. My mother had written it down on a piece of paper and left it on my bed. A boy on one of the Major League teams had broken his arm and I was being brought up. I was to pick up my uniform in an office above Hill's drug store. But what team?

I grabbed my bike and raced into town. I was going to pitch in the majors. It had all paid off. I felt a little bad about leaving the Dodgers; they were a nice group of boys and our coach was happy to have me on his team. I was supposed to start the first game that next Saturday against the Braves. It would not be easy calling him with the news.

I also felt sorry for the boy who had broken his arm. What a letdown that must have been. But I refused to let myself dwell on these factors. I was getting my shot, and my excitement was beyond control.

There was a lady in the office when I arrived. The room had obviously been set up specifically as a clearing-house for all the teams; there were stacks of uniforms on a large table and others—tagged with boys' names—hanging on a rack. I told her my name and she began sifting through those on the rack, passing a couple of Elks, pausing briefly at a blue Kiwanis uniform to read the name on the tag.

"What team am I on?"

"I'll know that just as soon as I find your uniform," she said, passing by the Kiwanis one. "Here we go."

She pulled the uniform from the rack. It had green pinstripes and a green hat. Across the front of the shirt was number 14, and on the back were the letters: V.F.W. I couldn't believe it.

"Try this on. If it's too big I'll have to see about finding you another. Looks like it might do, though."

I went into the bathroom and put on the suit. The sleeves were a little long, as were the pants, but nothing my mother couldn't take care of. One thing I knew: There was no way I was walking out of there without that uniform, no matter how big it was. I tried on the hat. It fit perfectly. I stood there in front of the mirror, admiring the picture before me. All that was missing were the shoes and of course my glove. I was on the team and up to that point it was, without a doubt, the happiest moment of my life.

———

The second phone call came a couple of days later from my father. He had found a job and was renting a house. We were to pack up and leave in three weeks. As I walked to the armory that Saturday for our first game, I still clung to the hope that somehow we would stay. I had my glove and my uniform (I had to use tennis shoes instead of cleats, due to the cost. I would only be around for three games and it would be too late to join once we got to California, and I would surely grow out of them by the following year.), and I was about to pitch in the Major Leagues. Surely the rug would not be pulled out from under me at this point.

Our first game was against the Elks. I knew the pitcher on their team, a big kid—a friend of mine named Gus—who lived around the corner from us. Nobody was looking forward to facing him at the plate. He was a head taller than anyone on our team and had an incredible fastball. And he was wild.

It never occurred to me that someone else besides me would be pitching for us, but when our coach called out the starting line-up, I was not on it. I sat back on the dugout bench trying to hide my disappointment. Perhaps, I thought, I'll get called in to relieve, or maybe I'll start our second game. But after five innings of play and three pitching changes, I had still not played. (We only played six-inning games.)

As our team started to take the field for the sixth inning, our coach came up to me.

"Okay, you're in," he said and I popped off the bench, eager to play. But there was already someone on the mound. "Right field."

"But I'm a pitcher," I said.

"Not today you aren't."

I took the field—right field, bottom of the totem pole. No one ever wanted right field for there was rarely any action out there. Most of the boys were right handed and the natural tendency was to pull the ball to left or center field. But in a way, I was relieved. I really had never prepared for the outfield. Could I catch a fly ball? Would I know who to throw the ball to in a base-hit situation? If I wasn't going to pitch I might just as well be in right, or stay on the bench for that matter. The thought crossed my mind that at that very moment I could have been pitching against the Braves in the Minors and I began to wonder if I hadn't made the wrong choice.

Game one ended without me ever touching the baseball, as did game two. In the third game, I was sent once again into right field for the sixth inning. I had found out that every player on every team had to get a chance to play in every game. Right field was where they put us.

We were ahead, three-two, in the bottom of the sixth. There were two outs and they had runners on first and second. As I stood in the field, my mind wandered away. After all, there had yet to be a ball hit my way and children are not apt to concentrate any more than they have to. I had felt so proud that first day, showing up in my new uniform, and even taking the field that first game and hearing a few people in the stands calling out my name had given me a sense of belonging. Now, in our third game, stuck in right field, I felt...betrayed. Everyone on our team who wanted to pitch had been given an opportunity. Why hadn't I? Who were these other boys? A couple of them were good pitchers, but the others were no better than me, I was sure of it. Was there more to it than ability, even in Little League?

The second baseman yelled out to me but I couldn't make out exactly what he was saying, something about the cut-off man. He drew my attention back to the game as a left-handed batter stepped into the box. The coach's son was pitching. He had started the first game and gotten clobbered and had pitched in relief in the second game and now again in the third. It was his second year on the team. He went into his wind-up and delivered his first pitch and the boy promptly smacked it down the right field line. With two outs, both base runners were off and running at the crack of the bat, so that by the time I got to the ball, the first runner was rounding third. Our first baseman ran into the outfield and began calling to me to throw him the ball. But I had other plans.

I was not that deep and the base runner was not that fast. I had the ball in my hand and was determined to make at least one pitch in that uniform before leaving for California. I took two quick steps toward the infield and fired the ball over the first baseman's head. I knew I couldn't reach the plate in the air, so I picked a spot about ten feet in front of it as my target.

It was a beautiful throw, sailing on a line just inches above the first baseman—he must have thought I was throwing it to him, for he jumped high into the air to try and catch it, but missed—smacking down onto the chalk line between home and first, kicking up a cloud of white dust, and coming to rest at last in the catcher's mitt—a perfect strike—beating the base runner by three full strides. The boy slid into the plate and the umpire's arm shot into the air.

"You're out!" he yelled and the crowd in the stands jumped to their feet, screaming and waving their arms. It seemed there was more than one way to be a pitcher, after all. As I ran in, my teammates gathered around me, patting me on the back and yelling in my ear about the great throw. When I reached the dugout our manager came up to me.

"You forgot the cutoff man," he said.

"No, sir, I didn't forget him. I knew I could beat the runner"

"Oh, you knew it, did you?"

"Yes, sir. He was slow."

"This is a team sport, son. Next time, follow my instructions."

"Yes, sir, it won't happen again."

"No, I suppose it won't. Next Saturday, you're pitching."

No, I thought, I won't. Next Saturday I'll be in California. I thanked him, said nothing about our moving and left the dugout. I stopped to gaze out at the field. I could still see that throw hurling toward home plate. I knew the second it left my hand that it was perfect, that it would beat the runner and save the game. I considered all the games I wouldn't be playing in that summer, all the pitches I wouldn't be throwing, the cheers that would never fill my ears and then I thought of Neely. How many years had he waited for his opportunity, an opportunity that never presented itself? Where was he now? What would he say to me, right now? Come what may in California, on that afternoon in the little ballpark in my hometown, I felt happy to be alive. That would have to do for now.

TWENTY-FIVE

We left Illinois the second week of June, on a Sunday. I had made the long walk back to town the day before to turn in my uniform. My mother had pressed it and folded it neatly into a box for me to carry. I took forty minutes to make the twenty minute walk, hoping, like a convict on death row, for some last-minute reprieve. It was not to be. I set the box on the table and explained to the lady in charge that I was only leaving the team because we were moving. She was kind enough to let me keep the hat.

My uncle Charlie would be taking us to the train station. He had come by two days prior to our departure and picked up what little freight we were sending, to put on an earlier train. I kept out a shoebox of baseball cards and a few other personal items to carry with me.

My mother went through the house that morning double-checking all the rooms to make sure we hadn't forgotten anything. She had lived in that house over fifteen years, but if she felt any remorse in leaving it, it didn't show on her face. She had been in good spirits since the day of my father's phone call. To her, this change was an opportunity to start over. To me, it was the end of the world.

Peter came by to say good-bye and I gave him my sled and my bike. I would not need the sled, and the bike—like most of our furniture—was not worth the cost of transporting. We also had to say farewell to the dogs. Kelly went to an uncle's farm and Sport was given to John Matuzak. It was the only aspect of the move that bothered Frank.

A few sprinkles of rain began to fall as my uncle pulled into our driveway. We loaded our suitcases into the trunk of his Cadillac and while everyone was saying their good-byes I made one last trip into the house. I ran up the stairs to my room and began rifling through my drawers. I knew there was something I was forgetting, but the drawers were all empty. I looked under the bed, stripped now of its sheets and blankets, nothing there.

There came a tapping at the window and I turned, almost expecting to see snow falling, but the sprinkles had merely turned to rain. I stared out the window to the scene below. The Slovaks were preparing to leave for church and had come across the street to say good-bye. Mrs. Slovak handed my mother a small package, then gave her a hug and she and her husband departed, hand in hand, toward the church. Mrs. Grady slowly crossed her yard and hobbled up to my mother. They stood their talking for a minute or so, Mrs. Grady no doubt telling my mother all about California. Then Carol and my mother hugged. (She would be staying behind. She and Richard would marry in September and then join us in California.)

I could see Frank running up the street, having returned from Matuzak's house. Mary hopped into the back seat and Frank got in next to her. For a minute I imagined them all driving away and leaving me there; perhaps they had forgotten me; perhaps I wouldn't have to leave. Then my uncle honked the horn and I could see my mother looking up at me. She waved for me to come down and I moved away from the window.

I climbed over the banister and inched my way along to the middle. It seemed a long way down to the steps. I let go of one hand, then I suspended one leg into space and without giving it another thought, dropped half way down the steps, leaning into the steps as I fell, and landed unharmed.

———

I sat in the back with Frank and Mary. My mother rode in front—Martin in hand—next to Phoebie. As we pulled away I turned to look back at our house, recalling a story from the bible of a woman turning to salt, or stone—I wasn't sure which—for looking back, and for a second I actually felt a tinge of fear as I cranked my head; but no threat could have kept me from that final look.

I was struck by the construction of the house. I had never paid it much attention before. I had always thought of it as being made of brick, but now realized—for the first time—it was actually composition shingles, cut in a pattern like brick. And there were spots where pieces of it were missing, the black tarpaper showing through. I wanted to go back and touch it. I wanted to run through the porch once more, stick my head through the missing pane.

Carol and Mrs. Grady continued waving as we reached the end of the street. Then we turned the corner and they, along with our house, were gone.

As we passed St. Anthony's, the noon bells rang out; last mass of the day had started. I thought about all the hours I had spent sitting in a pew listening to sermons and I recalled Frank's altercation with Father Steven. It all seemed so long ago.

Then we turned up Clark Street. I hadn't been there since Christmas day. Despite a series of snow storms, I could not quite convince myself to make that journey, to spend the day traversing that incline knowing that whenever I looked up, there would be no hat and no Neely gazing out from his window. Now today, knowing it might be the very last time I ever passed by here, I wasn't sure I could muster the courage to look.

Charlie's car proceeded down the hill. What a difference there is between a sled and a Cadillac. There were no bumps in the road—or at least we couldn't feel them—no one sneaking up from behind to sabotage our ride. On this particular ride, life was reduced to comfort. I looked over to the hospital, to Neely's room, half expecting to see him waving his hat. I wondered who was in his room. Where were all the kids? Where was Neely's yellow hat?

"Stop the car!"

"What's wrong?"

"My bag! I forgot my bag!"

"What bag?" asked my mother.

"I left the bag with Neely's hat and book."

"It's in the trunk."

"No. It's in my closet."

"I took it out of the closet myself, Michael. It's in the trunk."

"No, mom, it's not. We have to go back."

Charlie pulled the car over to the curb and we hopped out. He opened the trunk and there it was just as my mother had said. I took the hat out and put it on and I grabbed my glove, too. We got back into the car and proceeded toward the station. All along, Frank had yet to say a word, but as we turned off Clark Street and headed up Main, a grin came over his face.

Up ahead of us, I could see Matuzak walking along the

sidewalk, headed in our direction. He smiled and waved as we passed him by. A little further up the rode there was another figure, squirming up against a tree. As we got closer, my mother saw the figure by the tree.

"Oh, my God," she said. "What...?

There, stripped to his underwear and tied to the tree, his arms extended along two branches, his legs bound at the ankles, was Rick Thornton, squirming and tearing at the ropes in a desperate attempt to free himself. His feet were buried under a mound of corn and pigeons had begun to gather and peck away at it. My mother looked back at us.

"Frank Carmello! Charlie, stop the car."

"No!" said Frank. "Don't stop."

"Frank, that's terrible," said my mother.

"We don't have much a time," said Charlie. "We don't want to miss the train."

A woman came out of her house and ran over to Thornton. Charlie had slowed down a little, but when he saw her he sped up again. Phoebie turned around and looked back at us. She was trying hard not to laugh.

"Oh, Frannnnkie. You're a bad boy. Why you do that?"

"There you go Mike. Just a little going away present," said Frank.

The sight of Thornton tied to that tree managed to lift my spirits, but in all honesty, I had not, in any small way, made peace with our departure. Hardscrabble had been my entire life, a life I had struggled to make as full as possible under less than ideal conditions.

Most of my family was taking the ride to the station with me, and I was happy and somewhat comforted by their presence, but we were headed into territories unknown, cut off from everything I held dear. A myriad of images crossed my mind: Peter, the Slovacs, my school, the Little League field, Kelly and Sport. All of them would be gone now, as if they too were dead and buried next to Neely.

As we pulled into the parking lot at the train station, I felt sick to my stomach and tried my best to put my mind elsewhere. The Dodgers would be in L.A. Maybe I would get to see them. Maybe my father would be happier in California. Maybe he and Frank would make peace.

But these thoughts were not up to the task at hand. As everyone got out of the car, I sat frozen, unable, or unwilling to move. Anna had said that someday I would have to find my place. I knew what she meant, and I knew that day was coming, but right now, this was my place, my life, back there, around the corner, down Clark Street.

I could hear my mother's voice calling to me from outside of the car to hurry up; we were going to be late. I looked down at my glove and thought of Neely and those few precious days we spent together. I reached into my back pocket and pulled out the baseball card with Neely's picture on it. What would he say, right now? What would he do? For just a moment, I swear I felt his presence there next to me in the car, as if he were nudging me toward the door, and a calmness swept over me. I took my sleeve and wiped away the tears, gave a slight tug on Neely's hat and climbed out of the car.

The light rain from earlier had stopped and beams of bright sunlight broke through the clouds. I raised my head to the sky and caught a few seconds of warmth upon my face. My mother handed me a small suitcase to carry and then she put her arm around me and smiled, and I smiled back. Frank said something about sitting by the window and then of course Mary said she wanted to sit by a window, too.

Up ahead, the conductor removed his hat, waved it gently

above his head and yelled out, "all aboard," and we hastened our pace toward the train.

It was time to go.

℘